Alasdair stood up and halted the applause. "I'd be honored to be Santa, and if I may, I'd like to propose Shona as Chief Elf. She's another islander returned home who does good work at the local hospital. I'm sure she'd make an excellent elf."

The expression on Shona's face turned from shock to disbelief to poorly disguised anger directed at him. "That's not funny, Alasdair."

"All those in favor..."

Alasdair enthusiastically raised his hand and grinned at her, knowing she couldn't turn them down without running the risk of public disapproval. Not everyone could pull off the stripy stockings, pointy ears and rosy cheeks ensemble, but he knew Shona would rock it. That was if she didn't batter him unconscious with a candy cane first.

She might hate him now, but it was his impromptu nomination that would give them that much-needed time together to talk.

Dear Reader,

Christmas is such an important time for families. Perhaps now more than ever.

Shona and Alasdair are beginning to realize having that support around when things get rough means everything. The once teenage sweethearts have a lot of history to work through before they can learn to trust again. For an A&E nurse and a member of the local lifeboat crew, things are never going to be plain sailing. Especially during the winter!

I hope you enjoy my festive story because I loved writing it.

It's been a difficult time for us all recently, and I hope you and your loved ones are safe and well.

Merry Christmas!

Love,

Karin xx

THE NURSE'S CHRISTMAS HERO

KARIN BAINE

HARLEQUIN
MEDICAL
ROMANCE

HARLEQUIN®
MEDICAL ROMANCE™

Recycling programs
for this product may
not exist in your area.

ISBN-13: 978-1-335-40891-4

The Nurse's Christmas Hero

Copyright © 2021 by Karin Baine

This edition published by arrangement with Harlequin Books S.A.

For questions and comments about the quality of this book, please contact us at CustomerService@Harlequin.com.

Harlequin Enterprises ULC
22 Adelaide St. West, 40th Floor
Toronto, Ontario M5H 4E3, Canada
www.Harlequin.com

Printed in U.S.A.

Karin Baine lives in Northern Ireland with her husband, two sons and her out-of-control notebook collection. Her mother's and her grandmother's vast collection of books inspired her love of reading and her dream of becoming a Harlequin author. Now she can tell people she has a *proper* job! You can follow Karin on Twitter, @karinbaine1, or visit her website for the latest news—karinbaine.com.

Books by Karin Baine

Harlequin Medical Romance

Pups that Make Miracles
Their One-Night Christmas Gift

Single Dad Docs
The Single Dad's Proposal

Paddington Children's Hospital
Falling for the Foster Mom

From Fling to Wedding Ring
Midwife Under the Mistletoe
Their One-Night Twin Surprise
Healed by Their Unexpected Family
Reunion with His Surgeon Princess
One Night with Her Italian Doc
The Surgeon and the Princess

Visit the Author Profile page
at Harlequin.com for more titles.

For all the key workers and emergency services
who have worked tirelessly to keep us safe xx

**Praise for
Karin Baine**

"Emotionally enchanting! The story was fast-paced, emotionally charged and oh so satisfying!"
—*Goodreads* on *Their One-Night Twin Surprise*

CHAPTER ONE

'OF ALL THE people I hoped I'd never see again…'
Shona's instant reaction to setting eyes on Alasdair Murray was to lash out. Regardless of the
tattoo her heart was beating at the sight of him
again after a lifetime apart.

'That's one hell of a bedside manner you've
got there, Nurse Wallace.' He was actually grinning at her, without apparent remorse or shame
on his part. No sign of apology for the teen
trauma he'd caused her so long ago. Just a smile
and a reminder of how devilishly handsome
he was.

The mop of unruly dark curls, and those
navy-blue eyes, matched with the shadow of
masculine stubble, was as devastating to her
peace of mind as ever.

'It's Nurse Kirk now,' she bristled, hating that
he'd intruded into her life again and ambushed
her at work. It was always going to be a possibility, one of the cons she'd considered before

returning to Braelin Island off the west coast of Scotland. She'd hoped to avoid him for a while, but no, it was her luck to run into him on literally her first shift at the local hospital.

'Oh, yes. I forgot. You married. Insanely young.' There was no disguising the sneer in his tone at her life decisions. It would be easy to cut down his smugness with the use of one word. Widow.

Except this wasn't the time or the place to get into her personal affairs.

She glanced at her notes. 'You don't look like ten-year-old Eli Watts. So, if you wouldn't mind letting me get on with my job…'

Despite her attempt to dismiss him out of her way, he remained rooted in her path.

'Eli Watts,' Shona called again into the A&E waiting room.

A little red head peered out from behind Alasdair. 'That's me.'

'He…he's with you?' She glanced at her well-built childhood crush, then at the petite child he'd been blocking with his man bulk.

'Yes. No. I mean, I brought him here. He fell, down by the boathouse, and I was on my way home, so I thought I'd bring him in. I've phoned his parents but I'll wait with him until they get here.'

Great. In the meantime, she was stuck with him loitering around here.

'Okay, Eli, why don't you come with me and I'll get you triaged?' From the notes and the bloodied dressing on his leg, she could already tell it would take more than a sticking plaster.

She let them go into the triage room ahead of her and directed the boy onto the hospital trolley.

'He's going to need a few stitches,' Alasdair, the boy's self-appointed guardian, informed her.

She ignored him. 'How did you hurt yourself, Eli?'

'I was climbing on the rocks and slipped on some seaweed. There was a lot of blood.' Young Eli looked suddenly very pale and faint as the shock of his injury began to set in.

'Why don't you lie back and take some nice deep breaths? I'll clean this up for you.' Although the gash on his leg was deep, someone had done a good job of patching him up. 'Is this your handiwork?'

'Ah, yeah. I was a paramedic in Glasgow for a while.' This brief insight into Alasdair's history widened Shona's eyes and her view of him.

'Local bad boy done good, huh?' For as long as she'd known him, he'd had that reputation as the neighbourhood troublemaker, frequently suspended from school, breaking and entering, petty theft… Everyone had expected him to end up in jail. Except her.

'Something like that.'

She'd seen beyond the bravado. When they'd hung out together as kids, she'd witnessed a vulnerability in him she doubted anyone else had ever taken the time to uncover. It shouldn't surprise her that he'd managed to divert away from the path others had predicted for him. He'd always said he didn't want to end up a loser like his father.

In a weird way she was proud of him and the man he'd become. So she forced herself to remember the last time she'd spoken to him, giving herself permission to keep on hating him.

'Eli, I'm just going to clean your leg and change the dressing for you before you see the doctor. I'm afraid you are going to need a few stitches.' Her patient remained stoic as she delivered the bad news.

'You'll be fine, big man. The doctor will numb your leg before he stitches it.' Alasdair stepped up to the side of the bed to offer some big-brother-style reassurance.

Shona wondered if he was still in the medical profession in some way. The hospital was small, as was the island, so running into each other seemed inevitable. She wasn't comfortable with the idea.

'I'm sure I'm the last person you expected to see today.' After their last encounter he should have been too ashamed of himself to even look her in the eye. He didn't look anything of the sort.

Alasdair probably didn't even remember the cruel things he'd said to her in front of the whole school. Why should he? It was doubtful he'd given her a second thought since he'd made it clear her feelings towards him were entirely un-reciprocated.

'Not really. I moved back five years ago for a new start. I see people coming and going all the time.'

Why had he moved back to Braelin? Had he come back alone or with someone else? Why had he felt the need to start over?

Perhaps she wasn't the only one who'd had a tough time in their personal life. She really should have quizzed her sister more on the life and times of Alasdair Murray.

'I would've thought Braelin was the last place you'd find that.' Shona finished dressing Eli's wound and deposited the soiled one in the bin.

'True, true, but the devil you know and all that.' Alasdair's chuckle awakened a whole lot of new memories for her. The first time she'd heard him laugh so heartily was when she'd locked herself out of the house and he'd caught her trying to climb in through the window in an ungainly fashion. He'd teased her about copying his modus operandi, then proceeded to give her a boost with his hands planted firmly on her backside. Little wonder an impressionable teenage girl had assumed he was interested in her as more than his next-door neighbour.

They'd seen a lot of each other that summer, more so after her father had died. He'd gone out fishing and never returned. Shona really thought her world had ended that night. Her father had been her rock—her provider, comforter and confidant. The loss had been too great for her to bear and it was Alasdair who'd saved her from the pit of despair.

He'd done his best to cheer her up, walking with her on the beach. Letting her cry on his shoulder. Giving her a kick up the backside when she could barely drag herself out of bed. Teaching her how to skim stones and laughing at her pathetic attempts to replicate his triumphs when her stones hit the water with a 'plop' and sank without trace. Alasdair had been there for her and it had inevitably turned into more. At least for her.

Those had been the days when she'd thought they were enjoying each other's company, forming a bond. The highlight of her days had been in his arms, kissing and awakening feelings she'd never experienced before. Only to realise he wasn't as invested in their blossoming relationship as she was. He'd stood her up on one of the most important nights of her life, then rejected her so publicly at school.

She'd felt abandoned by Alasdair. He'd seen how devastated she'd been by her father's death. She was afraid of what her life would be without him in it. Her safe, constant guardian had gone and at times it seemed as though she was the one drowning, struggling to breathe without him to look after her. When Alasdair had hugged her, told her everything would be all right, she'd believed he would be the new constant in her life. Perhaps it was a lot to expect from a teenage boy, but when he'd disappeared out of her life too it was akin to another bereavement. Yes, she'd had her mum and Chrissie, but she'd been a daddy's girl. Then Alasdair's girl. Then no one's girl.

When Iain had come along, he'd filled that void in her life, offering the love, stability and support she'd longed for from a male figure. Only now he was gone too and she was right back to square one. This time she was determined to make it on her own and forgo the heartache and trauma of losing anyone else. Her family was all she needed.

All that teenage angst and drama surrounding

her and Alasdair should be consigned to the past along with terrible hairstyles and fashion fails.

If only it didn't continue to bother her about the reasons behind his hurtful behaviour towards her in the end.

'That's you all done for now, Eli. If you'd just like to take a seat out in the waiting room again the doctor will see you soon.' She knew she sounded much too happy to be seeing them out again but Alasdair was never going to be conducive to her having the quiet life she'd hoped to return to here.

When Iain had offered her a life away from the small community it had seemed an exciting prospect. He'd been a young, successful entrepreneur who'd come to the island with a view to building on their tourist industry. His plans to develop some of the land into a spa retreat hadn't gone down well with the locals but Shona had been impressed with his ambition. He'd asked her out after meeting her at the local pub and had showered her with compliments and expensive gifts. After everything that had gone on with Alasdair, her head had been easily turned by talk of life in the city and the prospect of a stable relationship.

Marriage to an older man had been romantic to an impressionable, grieving eighteen-year-old who'd already been burned by love once.

She had no desire to keep repeating the mistake until she found 'the one', and finding someone to settle down with at such an early age was everything she'd wanted. Iain was financially secure, openly declared his feelings for her and, compared to Alasdair, was a safe bet. Perhaps he'd even been a replacement father figure in her life, even though she hadn't realised it at the time.

Since then, she'd come to wonder about the person she might've been if she hadn't been in a hurry to get off the island.

Iain had encouraged her interest in nursing when they'd moved to Edinburgh, but she'd studied as a married woman, not as part of the student community, missing out on the social aspect and personal growth that probably went hand in hand in college life. She'd jumped straight into being part of a couple, without exploring the person she was in her own right. It was only since Iain's death that she was beginning to find out.

With their mother's death eight years prior, Chrissie and her twin daughters were the only family Shona had left. She'd jumped at the offer to go and stay with them, hoping to rediscover the Shona she'd used to be before marriage, city life and grief had worn her down. She had no intention of morphing back into that heartbroken teenager mooning after a lost cause.

Hopefully she wouldn't have to see him too often.

'Thanks, Shona. It was good to catch up. I'm sure we'll be seeing each other around.' He hovered in the doorway, preventing her from shutting him out altogether.

'Not necessarily,' she said, striving for the frosty air of someone who didn't care.

'We tend to get more emergency calls over the winter months.'

Now she was the one with her head cocked to the side, waiting for an explanation. 'You're still working as a paramedic?' Her heart kamikazed into the pit of her stomach.

'I'm not, but the lifeboat crew liaise quite a bit with hospital staff.'

'Lifeboat crew?'

'Yeah, I'm the station coxswain and mechanic over at the boathouse. Still saving lives, just in a different way.' He was grinning as her hand turned white clutching the door handle behind her.

'Good for you,' was all she managed to squeak out before closing the door in his face. She leaned her head back on the wooden barrier between them and closed her eyes. This hadn't been part of her plan. Neither seeing him nor reacting so emotionally to someone she should've forgotten long ago.

If she didn't love her new job and her family so much, she'd flee as she'd done at eighteen. Only next time she wouldn't marry the first man who asked, just to forget Alasdair Damn Murray.

Clearly Shona had neither forgiven nor forgotten him. Having first-hand confirmation that there was an area of his past which hadn't been laid to rest weighed heavily on Alasdair's heart. He'd only said the things he'd said, done the things he'd done, because he'd known he wasn't good enough for her.

With adult hindsight he could see he'd caused more hurt that way, but even if she heard him out now it wouldn't make any difference. The damage had been done a long time ago. They were strangers who'd led different lives down different paths and explaining his actions wasn't going to change anything.

He'd known Shona was back on the island alone and working at the hospital. Her return was the most exciting news to hit Braelin since Mr Peterson had bought a motorhome at the start of the summer.

Alasdair's first instinct had been to run to the hospital and apologise to her for everything, the

way he'd done with everyone else he'd wronged
when he'd come home. It had taken some time
to convince the residents with long memories
that he'd changed. Joining the lifeboat crew
had been pivotal in changing people's opinions
about him. The guys at the boathouse were at
the very heart of the community, so he'd made
sure to take part in all fundraising events to get
to know everyone again. The position he held
in the crew made it vital for the Braelin inhabitants to trust him.

Some day the fishermen in trouble at sea, or
the kids who'd swum out far beyond their capa-
bilities, might have to rely on him to save their
lives. There was no room for doubt. With Shona
he already knew it was going to take more than
a tour of the boatshed and a slice of homemade
cake to get her onside.

Young Eli's accident had provided Alasdair
with the opening he needed. At her place of
work, in the presence of a child, she hadn't been
able to tell him exactly what she thought of him.
Now that they'd had one brief, terse exchange,
he was hoping they'd get to speak again. Not
least because he was curious about her reason
for returning to Braelin too. Especially to live
with her sister and nieces and not a significant
other. He shouldn't have been pleased to find
out that tidbit when he knew how much break-

ups sucked, divorces even more so, he assumed, but he'd been glad she'd come back alone. It meant they had one thing in common.

Her long red hair had been tied up today into a work-efficient ponytail, but he remembered it blowing around her freckled face in the Scottish wilds. Her hazel eyes were framed by mascara-tinted lashes and her lips were shiny with gloss, but she was still his Shona. A combination he was already having trouble erasing from his memory.

'Eli? Come this way, please.' The doctor in green scrubs appeared and summoned his next patient. Alasdair went with him. Although the boy had braved it out to this point, he suspected some of that machismo could have been for Shona's benefit.

'All right, Doc? This one took a chunk out of his leg down on the rocks. I'm being chaperone until his parents get here.' Alasdair rested his hand on Eli's shoulder to let him know he wasn't alone. He knew what it was to have to come here alone and frightened, get stitched back together and sent back home. Except his parents had never turned up at any point, or cared. His mother had long abandoned them by the time he was Eli's age, but his father's absence had been down to complete uninterest. Some of his visits and injuries had been his own fault, others a punishment for alleged wrongdoing, but that was part of the past he was trying to leave behind.

'Hi, Al. Good to see you, pal. How's your dad doing these days?' Like most people on the island the doctor was aware of his father's declining health. The main reason for his homecoming.

Despite all his father's failings and their turbulent relationship, he was Alasdair's only family. They'd only had each other after his mother had abandoned them both when he was little, being part of a family apparently too stifling for a woman who'd struggled to fit into island life, according to the stories he'd heard.

He had the opposite point of view. It was something he longed to be part of and for a while he'd been led to believe it was in his immediate future. Until his girlfriend, Natasha, had changed her mind and made sure that wasn't going to happen. Aborting their baby without a discussion. Their relationship hadn't survived that betrayal and his life had suddenly become empty and void of possibility.

New start or second chance, Braelin was where he'd needed to be. Away from the shattered dreams of the family he'd never had, to reconnect with the one he did have. He'd reached out an olive branch to his father, regardless of how terrible their relationship had been. He was the only family Alasdair had, and even then he didn't know for how much longer.

'He has good days and bad days.'

The doctor nodded his head. 'Dementia is a cruel illness. It takes a toll on everyone.'

'Aye. At least he was more with it the last time I saw him. Enough to tell me I needed a shave and a haircut.' The visits to the nursing home were stressful, at times painful, but Alasdair would be there until the end. He might not get the chance to be the father he'd aspired to be, or to having, but he could be a good son. When his time came, he'd have no regrets or need to make amends. Except where Shona was concerned.

Slipping back in time for father and son didn't entail reminiscing about the happy times together. Those days had been filled with rows, broken ornaments and the odd punch thrown in for good measure. The good days now simply meant he managed to dodge anything physical thrown at him. Usually thanks to the help of the care home staff and sedatives.

'Now, young man, let me see that leg.'

Eli did as the doctor asked and Alasdair could feel the tension in the boy's body from across the room.

'You're going to freeze that leg before you get

the needle out, aren't you, Doctor?' He wanted to reassure Eli it wouldn't be as painful as he was probably imagining.

The doctor advanced towards the child propped up on the hospital bed. 'That's right. Just a small scratch…and we're done.' Eli sucked in a quick breath as the anaesthetic was administered to numb the area.

'That wasn't so bad, was it?' Alasdair gave him a thumbs-up and received a wavering smile in return.

In order to distract Eli, Alasdair and the doctor kept him engaged on the subject of his beloved football team until he was ready to be sutured.

'You'll have to keep the dressing dry and come back to get those stitches out. I'll see you next week,' the doctor promised Eli, then turned to Alasdair. 'I'll likely see you sooner than I'd prefer. No offence.'

'None taken.' It was the nature of their jobs that their paths only usually crossed in dramatic and often traumatic circumstances.

The adrenaline rush of a call-out for Alasdair often meant life or death for whoever was in need of his services. He never lost track of that thought. The job wasn't about his ego, erasing his past, or ingratiating himself with the community. There was no room for selfishness when it came to saving lives.

The three shook hands and on returning to the waiting room Eli was reunited with his parents.

'I had to get stitches, Mum.' The patient was keen to show off his war wound and share his adventures.

'What have I told you about playing down on the rocks by yourself? It's dangerous and your gran didn't know where you'd got to.' Eli's mother scolded him before grabbing him into a hug, clearly thankful it hadn't been anything more serious.

'Thanks for helping him and bringing him down here for us, Alasdair.' His father slapped Alasdair amicably on the back.

'No problem. I was clocking off for the day anyway.'

'Well, next time you're in the pub the drinks are on me.'

'Done.' They shook hands and Alasdair relinquished responsibility of the absconder. Compared to the things Alasdair had got up to at that age, going AWOL from a grandparent's house was a minor infraction.

He was sure he'd been in trouble for much worse during his primary school days. Stealing out of his classmates' lunchboxes had been a frequent crime. Looking back on that dirty, unkempt child in his second-hand, too small uniform, he couldn't help but pity him. He'd already been written off by his father and the teachers at school as a bad egg. It never occurred to them he'd been thieving out of necessity to fill an empty belly.

Even if anyone had given him the chance to explain his actions, he would have been too embarrassed to tell the truth. That there was no food in the house and his father forgot he was even there most of the time. In his eyes, boys needed to be tough. Especially those whose mothers had run off and left them to fend for themselves. In his eyes, it was Alasdair's fault his wife had run out on them, and he'd been punishing him for it ever since.

'You're the reason she's gone. All that whining and neediness drove her away. Just because I'm stuck with you, doesn't mean I'm going to baby you.' True to his word, Max Murray had treated his son as an inconvenience from that day, when he bothered to acknowledge him at all.

Alasdair hadn't understood his own behaviour then, never mind that of his parents. Now he knew it was the survival instinct of a neglected child which had been behind his young life of petty crime.

At one time he'd have eyed the happy reunion of Eli and his parents with a mixture of curiosity and a tinge of jealousy because he had no experience of that kind of relationship. Now it held a longing, a tidal wave of 'what ifs' for the family unit he'd once hoped to have too.

In moving away from the island and the preconceived notions of his character, training for a respected position in society, he'd done his best not to become another of the Murray men. According to history, they hadn't amounted to much other than casual labourers and full-time drinkers.

Despite his efforts, Alasdair hadn't been good enough for Natasha anyway. Perhaps it was a defective gene which rendered him unlovable, handed down from generations of men who only thought of themselves. How else could he explain his girlfriend getting rid of his baby, only to start a family with someone else?

For someone to have gone to such extraordinary lengths to avoid a life with him, causing him so much pain in the process, had taught him a lesson: not to give so much of himself, to love so completely, or to even share his life with anyone. It saved a lot of heartache all round for him just to accept he was destined to be alone.

What had happened with Shona had set the tone for all ensuing relationships. It had simply taken him a long time to realise he was still that loser teenager at heart.

'Are you still here?' Shona's sharp observation cut deep into his introspection.

'I…er…we're just leaving.'

'Uh-huh?' She folded her arms and narrowed her gaze at him. 'I think you'll find the others have already gone.'

At the tilt of her head he watched the family disappear out of the automatic doors. He'd been so deep in conversation with his personal demons he'd lost his excuse for sticking around. Shona knew it too.

'Sorry. I must've been miles away.'

'Is there anything else I can help you with?' Despite the question, she'd already turned away from him, towards the rest of the walking wounded in the waiting room.

'You know, I don't remember you being this cold, Shona.' He'd had similar responses from other islanders, but her blatant rejection irked him more than most.

'No? I wonder what on earth could have happened to make me this way?' she said through gritted teeth, and waved the next patient through to Triage.

He deserved that. All Alasdair could do was pray the kind, loving girl he'd known hadn't turned into this ice maiden because of something stupid he'd done a lifetime ago. Hopefully, this side of her was reserved for him only and in time he'd win her back around too.

'I'll see you around, Shona.'

She turned her attention back to him with a bright smile. 'I sincerely hope not.'

This was one apology he was going to have to work extra hard at to gain forgiveness.

CHAPTER TWO

'YOU'VE SEEN HIM, THEN?' Chrissie, Shona's younger sister, bundled her blonde-haired twin toddlers through the back door into the kitchen.

She was a Braelin lifer. Someone who'd never left the island and took odd jobs where she could. When their mother had been taken ill, she'd moved into their childhood home to look after her. Her death had hit them hard but had been expected and made it somewhat easier to come to terms with than their father's. Since then she'd been working as a classroom assistant at the local primary school. Only to make the classic mistake of falling for someone who'd been a summer worker at the nearby hotel. A passionate affair which Chrissie had expected to last for ever. Jake, however, had only seen it as a holiday fling and had promptly forgotten about her once he'd gone back home. Not even the prospect of becoming a father had changed his mind, leaving Chrissie as a single mother to beautiful Matilda and Marie, almost since the time of conception.

'What? Who? How did you know?' The hustle and bustle of the young family returning home snapped Shona out of her daze at the sink. The water in the washing-up bowl was cold now, her fingers wrinkled after being immersed in it for so long.

'Alasdair Murray. He's the only one who could possibly annoy you so much you're trying to scrub the pattern off my best dishes.'

Shona stared at the long-forgotten plate in her hand before finally setting it in the dish rack. 'Sorry. I got distracted.'

'I'll say. He doesn't live there any more, you know.' With well-practised moves, Chrissie wrangled the girls out of their coats and winter wellies. They ran on ahead as fast as their sock-clad feet would take them and turned on the television.

Shona had been caught staring at the neighbouring cottage, remembering the young Alasdair who'd lived there once. Despite having met the newly-wed couple who'd made it their home recently, she wondered if she'd still been half hoping to catch a glimpse of him there. She'd stood at this window on many a night, waiting to see him coming or going, usually followed by the sound of a slamming door and raised voices.

'He came into work today.'

'And? I've been waiting for you to mention him since you came back. I know you haven't forgotten what he did to you any more than I have.'

'And I triaged the young boy he'd brought in before they saw the doctor.' Skimping on the details of their encounter earned Shona a hard stare from her unamused sibling. She was surprised Chrissie remembered the school scandal when she'd barely been a teen herself at the time. It didn't bode well for her hope that everyone who hadn't been personally humiliated that day would have forgotten that particular incident.

'You really ought to be over all that teenage angst by now, Sis. It was a long time ago and you've been through a lot worse since.' The only thing worse than Chrissie's unimpressed face was her sympathetic head-tilt. Shona had had enough of that to last a lifetime. Losing a husband instantly made her a figure of pity that no one had been able to see past for the better part of a year.

'I thought I was over it. Until I saw him again. I don't know, all of those feelings just came flooding back again.' Embarrassment, despair and, worst of all, that longing for him. Guilt immediately made itself known, reminding her she was still in mourning for her late husband. Whilst it was true that she missed Iain's company, hated the cruelty of cancer which had robbed him of his future, their last years together had been more about friendship than a passionate, all-consuming love.

When they'd married, Shona had been looking for a way off the island. She'd needed someone to take care of her, to want her. In hindsight she'd confused that for love. They'd been a good team, but they'd never had that explosive, all-consuming chemistry she and Alasdair had once had.

Shona had assumed the role of a wife, but when Iain died she'd had to rediscover who she was beyond that. Their friends were his from work. The house they owned was in the town where he'd been born and raised. There was no trace of her life before their wedding.

It had begun to eat away at her until she made the decision to move back to Braelin. The one place she remembered being truly happy. For a while. Perhaps she'd wanted to recapture those memories, that sense of belonging. Whatever it was that had drawn her back, she was happy to be in familiar surroundings among people she'd known growing up. Running into Alasdair had upset everything, knocked her off-kilter and dislodged some of the unhappier times she'd spent here from her brain.

'What happened? Did you confront him about what he did? Slap him? Burst into hysterical tears and marry the first man you stumbled across? Again?' Chrissie helped herself to one of the Christmas cookies cooling on the rack which Shona hadn't long taken out of the oven.

'Ha-ha-not-so-ha. You know that's not what happened. Not entirely. And it definitely didn't happen like that today.' There was some truth in the teasing, but it would be disrespectful to Iain to admit it and diminish the basis of their marriage. Something she might think but would never say to her sister.

'Ooh, did something else happen, then? Did you run into each other's arms like two long-lost lovers finally reunited?' Chrissie was still smiling as she crunched on her cookie. Shona was tempted to shove another one in her face.

'I thought I was perfectly civil to him. Under the circumstances.'

Chrissie raised her eyebrows. 'Alasdair disagreed?'

Shona frowned as she recalled his words. 'He called me cold.'

It wasn't the impression she wanted to give, even if it was to someone who deserved an entire blizzard blowing around him at full force.

Laughter wasn't the response she expected after recounting the event either.

'Sounds as though you pitched it just right. You're over him but you haven't forgiven him. That should give Mr Murray something to think about before he disses my big sis again. Way to go, Sho.'

'I guess.' Maybe he'd go out of his way to avoid her in future now he knew he wasn't dealing with the soft-natured girl he'd once known. She'd prefer that to the heart-jolting reaction she'd had upon seeing him again and being confronted by her past.

'These are really good.' A spray of crumbs emitted from Chrissie's mouth as she munched on another biscuit.

'Hey. Leave some for tonight. You don't want to go into the community centre empty-handed.' With Chrissie's time fully accounted for with the twins and work, Shona had volunteered to do a bit of baking for her. There was a meeting tonight to organise the island's annual Winter Wonderland event. Every year the islanders transformed Braelin into a festive paradise with craft stalls, ice sculptures and Santa Claus welcoming day trippers from the mainland.

It was an important fundraiser for the community. Hence the oh-so-important committee meeting. Those hefty decisions being made for the future needed to be fuelled with gallons of tea and mountains of home-baked goods. Attendees were required to contribute to the residents' expanding waistlines during the Christmas season.

'About that—'

Shona didn't like the sound of the excuse beginning to form on her sister's lips. 'What?'

'I'm really tired and the twins have the start of a cold. I don't want to leave them. I thought maybe you could go tonight in my place.'

Shona quickly dried her hands on a tea towel. 'No way, Chrissie. I don't mind helping with the housework or babysitting but I absolutely draw the line at that.' She was trying to ease herself gently back into island life. Standing in for her sister at the Christmas committee meeting was like being plunged head-first into the deep end.

'Pretty please.' Chrissie pouted and hugged Shona, who left her arms hanging very firmly by her sides.

'This isn't fair, you know.' Since her sister had let her move in she'd found it difficult to say no to anything when she was so grateful to have family in her life again. Even if on this occasion she'd be wishing to be somewhere else for the duration of the evening.

'I know, but you love me and you'd do anything for your baby sister.' Chrissie batted her eyelashes, knowing full well every word was true.

'I must do to even contemplate doing this for you,' Shona muttered.

Talking about who got the pitch closest to the public toilet for their needlework stall was not how she'd planned to spend her evening. Yet it would be quieter than the squealing twins during their power hour before bedtime.

'In which case you'd best get a move on. You don't want to be late.' Chrissie patted her on the cheek.

A glance at the kitchen clock told Shona there was no time to shower or change before turning up as her sister's substitute.

'Help me box these up. I don't want to be stumbling in halfway through the meeting. That's not going to look good for either of us.'

They worked together to get the sugary treats packed up and Shona managed to grab her coat before Chrissie pushed her out of the door.

'Save one for Alasdair,' she cackled behind her. 'He's usually the first one to put the kettle on.'

Alasdair hadn't been looking forward to the committee meeting but as head of the lifeboat crew he had a duty to represent their section of the community. Some of the funds raised during the Wonderland festivities were donated to the upkeep of the boats. Everything, including his wages, was funded by public donations. It was in everyone's best interests to make the event a success.

'We'll take submissions for pitches as usual, but long-serving members of the community will be allocated first preference of location.' The bespectacled chairman of the Christmas committee and head of the local primary school had the floor.

The rest of those present were sitting in a circle of hard plastic chairs around him. A lot of the items on the agenda weren't relevant to Alasdair or his crew and he switched off after a while when it came to debating the choice of Christmas carols for the choir. His mind drifted back over the events of today. With the memory of one person standing out in particular: Shona.

It wasn't the way he'd imagined seeing her again. No 'meet cute' where they'd laugh about the past and how silly they'd been as kids. He was more disturbed by her reaction to him than anyone else's on the island. Probably because she'd been the one person who'd always believed in him and who'd given him chance after chance. He hated that he'd let her down more than anyone else.

Then there she was, bustling into the room, apologising for being late and making a racket as she unloaded her contribution of treats to the table at the side of the room.

'You haven't missed too much. We were just going over the number of stalls we have allocated this year and the programme for the choir. It's Shona, isn't it? Chrissie's sister? Take a seat.' Eric, the chairman, welcomed her while the rest of the group were breaking their necks trying to see who he was talking to.

Alasdair pulled over a chair into the space next to him. 'There's one here.'

'I'd rather stand, thanks,' she spat in his direction. Only to accept Eric's offer of his seat.

Okay. Alasdair was really going to have his work cut out to even get her to talk to him. Goodness knew how he was supposed to apologise so they could move past it. What he did know was that it had suddenly become his mission to win her forgiveness.

'Now we move on to that all-important subject of this year's Santa Claus. As you know, the person chosen to represent Christmas on Braelin must be an outstanding member of the community willing to devote himself to the role. Is there anyone you would like to put forward for this prestigious position?' Although Eric's comments were very tongue-in-cheek, Alasdair was aware of how coveted that role was after last year's shenanigans. He'd nearly had to break up a fist fight between the school's lollipop man and Frank from the corner shop.

'I'd like to propose Alasdair Murray this year.' Eli's dad, Tony Watts, was on his feet, stunning the room into silence.

'I don't think so, but thanks, Tony.' Alasdair's cheeks were on fire. It was a nice gesture, but he knew he'd burned his bridges a long time ago. There was no way they'd agree to let him hold the prized position.

Eric nodded his head. 'That's a good call. You've earned your place here, Alasdair. You have our respect and admiration for the work you do. I think you'd make a great Father Christmas. Can we have a show of hands to elect Alasdair Murray for Mr Claus this year?'

Alasdair watched, mouth open, face aflame, as hand after hand shot up in agreement. Everyone's except Shona's.

'I'm only standing in for my sister. I don't have a vote,' she explained when all eyes fell upon her.

That hurt and did detract a little of the pride he'd experienced at the nomination. She didn't know him. Not any more. He was determined to put that right.

'I'm sure Chrissie would agree. Vote carried. Alasdair is our new Santa Claus.' Eric started a round of applause which left him beaming at the accolade. It was confirmation he had turned his life and reputation around to find acceptance here. With one exception.

He stood up and halted the applause. 'I'm honoured, and if I may, I'd like to propose Shona as Chief Elf. She's another islander re-turned home who does good work at the local hospital. I'm sure she'd make an excellent elf.'

The expression on her face turned from shock, to disbelief, to poorly disguised anger directed at him. 'That's not funny, Alasdair.'

'All those in favour.' Eric ignored her protest and put his hand up, encouraging the others to follow suit.

Alasdair enthusiastically raised his hand too and grinned at her. She couldn't turn them down without running the risk of public disapproval. Chief Elf wasn't contested as hotly as the main gig. Not everyone could pull off the stripy stock-ings, pointy ears and rosy cheeks ensemble but he knew Shona would rock it. That was, if she didn't batter him unconscious with a candy cane first.

'Congratulations and welcome home, Shona.' Eric was shaking her hand as she continued glaring daggers at Alasdair. She might hate him now, but it was his impromptu nomination which would give them that much-needed time together to talk.

Shona lined up for her tea along with everyone else but only because she'd been carried there on a tide of congratulations and best wishes. Despite the smile she'd barely managed to hold in place, inside she was plotting whether to kill Chrissie or Alasdair first.

'Tea or coffee?' He was standing on the other side of the catering table pouring hot beverages as though he was some sort of do-gooder. Not the local bad boy everyone had used to keep their distance from. She wouldn't put it past him to have put something in the water to make them all forget the past. Well, she wouldn't be reeled in so easily by his new-found charm and long-lasting good looks. Not this time.

'Thanks for that, by the way. It would have been nice for you to have checked with me first. I do have a life, you know.' She nearly choked on the lie. Apart from working and babysitting she hadn't planned anything. The more she ventured out, interacted with people, the more they'd be interested in her reason for moving back. She wasn't ready to discuss her personal life or her grief. Now Alasdair was forcing her to come out of hiding for his own amusement.

'Really?' He said it as though he was fully aware that she'd completely immersed herself in domestic bliss with her family, swerving the outside world so far.

'I've just started work. I help my sister out with my nieces.' *Shut up*, she wanted to scream as she got flustered, spilling the milk into her tea. 'I work.'

'Yeah, you said that. I work too but there is life beyond the job. Maybe I'll see you at the local pub some time. Unless you're avoiding me?'

She wouldn't give him the satisfaction of confirming that was exactly what she'd been doing. 'I'm not seventeen. I don't waste time or energy thinking about you any more.' Lies.

'Did you make these, Shona? They're so cute. You're going to make a great elf. I remember when you and Alasdair here used to pal around as bairns. Isn't it funny how things work out?' Val from the post office had lifted Shona's offerings and handed them around. Alasdair picked out one of the melted snowmen biscuits.

'Hilarious,' she quipped as he took a bite. It would go against all of her medical ethics to hope the snowman's marshmallow head would swell and temporarily block Alasdair's airways.

It was disturbing how visceral her reaction to this man had become when she'd loved him once. She supposed that was how unrequited teenage love and public rejection manifested in adulthood. As much as she wasn't relishing the idea of this elf thing, perhaps their time together would give her some sort of closure.

Val moved on with the biscuits, leaving them alone again.

'Tell me what exactly you've got me roped into?' she asked, trying to find the positive in the situation; she did love Christmas. She was looking forward to spending it with Chrissie and the girls.

Her greatest regret was never having had children of her own. Iain hadn't wanted any, believing they should stay totally devoted only to each another. Young, naïve and in love, Shona would have agreed to anything to marry him. It was only later in the marriage she realised what she'd given up, but at least she could be a good auntie to her nieces now she was back in their lives.

'We'll cover that at the sub-committee meeting.'

'What?' She didn't think she had the motivation to do this night after night. She wasn't a committee person. That had been Iain. He'd enjoyed being part of everything, involved in all decision-making that might have impacted on his life. Shona preferred to be one of the sheep, going with the flow, doing whatever it took to live a quiet life. 'Can't you just give me the overview?'

Alasdair shook his head and fixed her with a hard, dark stare. 'Santa Claus takes his duties very seriously and so should his Chief Elf.'

Shona sighed. She'd have weeks of this nonsense to contend with now. Chrissie was going to bust a gut laughing when she found out.

'Okay. Who, what, where and when is this sub-committee thing?'

'Me, you at the pub tomorrow night at six o'clock. Ho, ho, ho. Merry Christmas.' Alasdair clutched his flat belly while practising being his jolly alter ego.

She knew there was no point in calling him out on this 'sub-committee' nonsense. He clearly enjoyed seeing her squirm, but she intended on playing him at his own game. She was going to be so nice to him he'd regret ever messing with her. Seventeen-year-old Shona was finally going to get her revenge. Or at least an explanation.

The only Christmas present she wanted this year was Alasdair Murray to finally get his comeuppance.

CHAPTER THREE

WITH THE MASS butterfly migration happening in Shona's belly, and her indecision over what to wear to meet Alasdair, this had all the markings of a first date when it couldn't have been further from the truth.

During last night's meeting at the community centre she hadn't given a thought about her old jeans and icing-sugar-dusted sweater. Now, though, she'd had so many outfit changes it warranted a natty pop song played over a movie montage. She'd even invited the opinions of the other female inhabitants of the house before settling on what she was wearing.

Marie had voted for her hospital scrubs before she'd had time to change. Whereas Tilly had been adamant she should wear the old wedding dress she'd been too sentimentally attached to get rid of during her move.

'I think a wedding dress might be a bit too much for a first date, sweetheart.'

'Chrissie, how many times do I have to tell you it's a meeting about this stupid Winter Wonderland thing? Stop stirring.' She'd been quick to correct her sister about the nature of tonight's appointment and had told her repeatedly she was duty-bound to go because of her Chief Elf status. A title Chrissie took great delight in addressing her as when the mood struck.

'It's been a year, Sho. You're allowed to look. We all like to look at Alasdair. He's a major hottie.' Chrissie had fanned herself with Tilly's artwork, which had been spread over Shona's bed along with the contents of her wardrobe and her spectating family.

'Yeah, well, he can't be all that hot if no one on the island wants him. No wedding ring either. I assume he's a bit of a player.' Shona told herself it was only human to be interested in what he'd been doing or who he'd been with since high school. He had no family that she knew about and was way too pretty to be single without a damned good reason.

'Honestly, I haven't seen or heard of him being with anyone since he came back. You must be special.' Chrissie had held up the wedding dress again and winked.

'Two words. Committee. Meeting,' Shona had reiterated, though her traitorous heart gave an extra beat at the prospect of seeing him on her own. Just as it had that night she'd believed they were going to be together for ever.

Shona couldn't be sure if it was the time of night or the ambience of romantic couples dining together which put her on edge. The only time she'd been here previously had been for Sunday lunch with Chrissie and the girls. This evening visit felt different.

The open fire was blazing in the hearth, the cosy atmosphere enhanced by the flickering candle centrepieces on the tables and the glow of warm white Christmas lights from the tree in the corner. The bar top and the mantelpiece were decorated with leafy garlands interspersed with red velvet bows, and the requisite Christmas music was playing over the speakers. It was the perfect setting for a festive dinner and only time would tell if the remainder of the evening would be as pleasant as the décor.

Alasdair was sitting by the window. When he saw her, he immediately got to his feet and waved her over.

'Hey, Shona, good to see you.'

'Like I had a choice.' Her foul mood rose once again, summoned by that rogue heartbeat making a reappearance.

'You could have cried off,' he said as they sat down.

'And ditch my first responsibility as Chief Elf? That wouldn't make me very popular, and you of all people should know how difficult that makes living here.' It was indiscreet, not to mention petty, to bring that up but she had to remind herself who she was dealing with here, what he was capable of, in case she started falling under his spell again.

He didn't react, continuing to study the menu until the waiter came to take their order.

'I'll have the scallops with black pudding and pea purée to start. Followed by...the sea bream with lemongrass and chilli, please.' Alasdair ordered first and closed his menu.

'Same, please.' Shona didn't usually go for seafood, at least not in city restaurants. Here, though, she'd sampled some of the freshest and tastiest food she'd ever had. She decided to be a little more adventurous in her choices tonight.

They ordered a bottle of wine and Alasdair poured them a glass of water each while they waited. 'You know that's not why we're here, right?'

She swallowed her sip of water, anticipating the rest of the evening with a sense of dread. With her hands resting in her lap, she tried to stop her knees from shaking so he wouldn't see he was capable of making her tremble with nerves.

'Coming back here, I had to face the consequences of a lot of my actions in the past. Something I was willing to do because I wanted to make amends and find a home here again. For the most part I've been able to do that. What I did and said to you was unforgivable.'

'It's all in the past.' Regardless of her own behaviour towards him recently, she attempted to dismiss the events when tears were already pricking her eyeballs. An involuntary reaction she'd developed in relation to that particular memory and one she didn't wish him to witness.

'Yes, but not forgiven, I've noted. I don't want you to hate me, Shona.'

'Why do you care? We haven't seen each other for…what? Fifteen years? You can't tell me this has been eating away at your conscience for all this time. I've hardly given you or what happened a second thought.' It was easier to perpetrate the lie than let him believe he'd affected her so deeply. That it had been playing on a loop in her brain since she'd set eyes on him again.

'I've thought about it a lot lately.' He gave her a coy look and she realised he'd been suffering a similar affliction to hers. 'Listen, we're living on an island, we're going to be working together and seeing a lot of each other. I'd prefer to clear the air.'

Shona inhaled a deep breath and let it out

slowly. 'Why did you do it? What made you say those things? Did you mean them?'

Over the course of those hot summer days and nights together she'd decided that he was 'the one'. They'd planned to spend the night together, and she'd been sure they were madly in love and destined to be together for ever. Alasdair had assured her his father would be at the pub that night and told her to come over. When she got there the place was in darkness and no one answered the door to her. Confused, she'd approached him in school the next day, where he'd yelled at her to leave him alone and stop following him around like a lovesick puppy. He'd told her in no uncertain terms that he wasn't interested and she should stop throwing herself at him. It had happened in the busy school corridor for everyone in their year to hear and mock her. At that age she'd felt as though her whole world had ended.

Alasdair's shoulders dropped and he ducked his head. 'I'm sorry. I was an idiot teen but had enough life experience to realise I'd never be good enough for you. We were kids who thought we were in love, but I had nothing to offer you. I didn't want to end up like my parents. With me a useless drunk who couldn't keep a job and you resenting me for making you a prisoner here.'

Shona's gut twisted at the utter injustice of

what he was telling her. His rejection had sent her running headlong into a marriage which should never have happened anyway. 'What changed overnight to make you think that? I thought we were in love.'

'Perhaps we were,' he said on a sigh. 'You have to understand what I had to put up with at home. Dad did go out that night but not before a tirade of abuse directed at me. I believed every word of it. He'd seen us together and laughed about it. I told him we were in love and that only made him mock me more, saying that I was punching way above my weight. That you'd open your eyes one day and see that I'd ruined your life the way I'd ruined my mum's. I had a vision of you pregnant right out of high school and my parents' history repeating all over again. I knew you'd end up resenting me anyway so I thought I may as well get it over with sooner rather than later.'

'You couldn't have shared your fears with me or had an actual, honest discussion about the future?' She could hardly get the words out past the ball of anger lodged in her throat. His father, who should have been nurturing him and building up his confidence, instead had made it his mission to tear Alasdair's self-esteem apart. Breaking her heart in the process. She could picture him now, sitting in the dark while she'd been knocking at the door, tears streaming down her face, wondering why he'd changed his mind about being with her.

Alasdair finished eating and carefully laid the cutlery back on his plate. A drink of water and a sigh later he finally responded. 'Teenage boys aren't developed enough to deal with that kind of emotional situation. In my head it was a straightforward decision. I'd make you hate me so you'd find someone who deserved you.'

Shona swallowed her forkful of food without chewing. 'My emotional development wasn't any further on than yours. I simply thought you didn't want me. That you'd never felt about me the way I'd felt about you.'

'Shona, you must have known exactly what you did to me every time we kissed.' Was it her imagination or had his voice dropped an octave until the gravelly baritone was bringing out goosebumps over her skin? Contradicted by the hot flush brought back by the memory.

'Something which you strenuously denied later, of course.' She steeled herself against the soft, squishy feelings he was trying to encourage inside her.

He shifted in his seat. 'Said with good intentions at the time. That's why I wanted to meet tonight and explain what I did. Who I was. A mixed-up kid. All of that stuff I got in trouble for—the break-ins, the stealing—it wasn't me simply living up to my hard man image. Things were tough at home. Mum had been gone so long I could've walked past her in the street and I wouldn't have recognised her. Dad, well, he was a mess after that. He didn't care about anything. Including me. I broke into houses to take food because there was none at home. I stole money to pay some of the bills that were coming in. I was trying to survive.'

It was clear to see he was ashamed of what he'd had to resort to in order simply to live. His eyes were conveying that pain and embarrassment so accurately it was painful to see.

'I know.'

He looked up at her, his downcast gaze now full of surprise. 'You knew?'

She reached her hand across the table to take his, just as she'd done when they were teenagers and she'd found him crying on the beach. He'd denied that too but she'd seen the tears before he'd angrily wiped them on the back of his sleeve.

'I witnessed enough rows, heard the slaps, punches and breakages to have some idea of what was going on.'

'The tough-guy exterior didn't work, huh?' That heartbreaking smile caused a hairline crack in Shona's defences.

He'd been in a bad situation at home and she'd been privy to a lot of it living next door. That was why she'd made allowances for him when other people wouldn't. Provided a listening ear when he'd needed one. Which was why the way he'd treated her had been such a betrayal of trust.

'Not with me.' She'd seen the frightened boy beyond the bravado and had admired his strength. He'd never told anyone what was going on at home or expected sympathy and leniency. Alasdair had accepted every punishment, each insult, as though he deserved them.

'You were a good friend to me. The only one I had.' Instead of giving her a warm glow, his words sparked that fire in her back to life.

'You hurt me, Alasdair.' That pain, like a vice squeezing her heart until she was sure she would die, was as strong now as it had been then.

He let out a heavy breath she imagined was laden with responsibility and guilt. 'I didn't go about things in the right way. Acted first, regretted it later, and believe me I did when I saw how much I'd hurt you. When you left Braelin I thought I'd done the right thing in letting you go but yes, my methods were questionable to say the least.'

'You don't say. I would've settled for being dumped literally any other way.'

'I thought I was protecting you.'

'Hmm.' It was hard to forgive everything on his say so after all this time of seeing his actions as the ultimate rejection. Even though she was looking back on that time now with a different perspective.

'I understand it might take some convincing for you to believe I'm a good, honest guy now. That's why I nominated you to be my elf. We'll spend enough time together for you to see it yourself.'

'Why is it so important to you? Not everyone in life has to be a fan.' It would be easier to keep on hating him rather than noticing how his eyes sparkled when he spoke or how the dimples around his mouth deepened when he smiled. She reminded herself she had absolutely not come back to fall into bad habits.

'Ah, but you did like me once. I simply want to make reparations. This island's too small to have someone hating on me. I can't have this on my conscience any more.'

'This is all about you, then?' She couldn't resist teasing when things were so serious between them and she had so much new information to process. He'd had strong feelings about her after all. Only someone in love would have wanted the best for her, regardless of what that meant for him. It meant all those angry, hurt emotions had been pointless. Perhaps if she'd stayed on the island they might've resolved things but she'd run at the first opportunity. Now she'd never know what could have been between them. It put an even sadder spin on those years they'd been apart.

'If tonight was about laying the past to rest you've succeeded. You apologised and I've accepted you were an immature child who didn't know how to express himself adequately. We've both grown up enough to work together without letting residual resentment get in the way.' She hoped. Along with any lingering feelings beginning to resurface.

'Thank you for that and agreeing to meet me tonight.' Alasdair held up his glass of wine for a toast. 'To us.'

It seemed too intimate a moment, perhaps even premature for their newly agreed truce. Shona amended it accordingly.

'Here's hoping we don't kill each other.' She clinked her glass to his, marvelling that he wasn't the beer-bottle-holding, leaning-on-the-bar kind of company she'd expected.

Then his pager went off and she realised why he wasn't knocking back the lager.

'Always on duty. It's a call-out. Sorry. I'm going to have to run.' He was already standing with one arm in his jacket. He dug into his pocket for his wallet then threw his credit card on the table. 'Order dessert, tea, coffee...whatever you want.'

Before she could tell him she didn't want anything he was gone. From her vantage point at the window she had a good view of the bay. As dark as it was outside, she could make out the swell of the waves before they crashed on the shore.

She shivered, picturing Alasdair and the rest of the crew setting off into that black night, outcome unknown.

After cancelling the rest of their meal, she paid the bill, courtesy of Alasdair. Getting her coat, she braved the cold night herself. It didn't sit right with her to go back to Chrissie's and continue her evening when the crew were facing goodness knew what out there. They were experienced, and had to be good at their jobs, but it wouldn't stop her worrying about the worst that could happen out there under cover of darkness.

Her father had died at sea and she hadn't been able to do anything about it. He'd gone out in a boat too and she'd never seen him again. That sense of powerlessness was the reason she'd gone into nursing. To help people and try to prevent their loved ones going through the loss she'd experienced. It was also the reason behind rushing into her marriage. She'd wanted security. A no-risk relationship where she wouldn't get hurt. Being reminded of Alasdair's career choice and the dangerous nature of it, she knew she'd been right to walk away from him the first time for her own peace of mind.

Shona pulled the hood of her coat up around her face to keep the icy wind out and tucked Alasdair's credit card into her purse. Before she knew it, she was heading towards the boat-house where the lights were still blazing, the boat bay empty. Despite their differences and time apart, she wouldn't be able to rest knowing his life could be in jeopardy. She had a need to do something useful. Even if it was only to pro-vide hot drinks to those returning from the cold.

She found the kitchen area, set out cups and waited for the kettle to boil.

Hours ticked by as she curled up in a nearby armchair. If she closed her eyes for a few min-utes she was sure she'd hear the crew when they made it back. Safely, she hoped.

Using her coat as a blanket and the arm of the chair for a pillow, she bedded down to wait. It was with thoughts of Alasdair's sparkling blue eyes and dimpled smile that she drifted off to sleep.

Every shout was accompanied by a rush of adrenaline, but Alasdair had experienced that before the call came in. From the second Shona had walked into the bar, in fact. If he thought she'd looked well last night, she was absolutely stunning tonight.

Even as he was bouncing across the waves, sea spray whipping against his face in the dark, he could picture her as she'd stood in the doorway. The figure-hugging black jeans and tailored polka-dot blouse had shown off the curves she'd developed since her teens, but the flames of red hair around her shoulders reminded him of the Shona he'd used to know. That fiery halo brightened any room and called to the teen in him who'd always been able to spot her in a crowd.

Once upon a time she'd been his friend, confidante and almost-lover, but he'd denied himself that ultimate pleasure. Performing the one selfless act he'd come to regret. He'd never get back what they'd once had but at least he'd been able to explain himself tonight. To be back on speaking terms with her was all he could have asked for. It was a shame the night had had to end so abruptly when he'd been keen to find out more about her life since high school. He'd have to put his interest on hold until he finished the job at hand and was safely back on dry land.

'Throw the line.' They'd reached the stricken fishing boat which had reported an injured crew member to the coastguard.

It was down to Alasdair and his men to tow the ship back and stabilise the patient for the coastguard. First, they had to tie the two boats together. Which was easier said than done with both being buffeted by the wind and the swell of the sea.

It took a few attempts before the crew of the stricken ship caught hold of the line and anchored to the lifeboat.

'I'm going over to assess the injury,' he told Greg, the second coxswain.

'It's rough out there. Maybe you should wait for the coastguard to get here.'

'It'll be fine. I've done this a hundred times.' A slight exaggeration but it wasn't his first high-octane, risky transfer from ship to ship. Plus, he was the one on board with the most medical experience.

Being on the lifeboats was as exhilarating as being a paramedic. Only with added peril. Perhaps the guilt from his past mixed with his tendency towards risky behaviour had led him down this noble career path. He was saving lives. There was nothing safe or boring about his life. At least not in his work life. His personal life had been staid since his ex. Something which had perked up with Shona back on the scene.

Sure, she might never again think of him in

that way she had when they'd used to make out down on the beach. However, the fact he was even thinking about another woman in that way was a revelation.

He got his head, and the rest of his body, back on board the boat to negotiate the transfer, surfing between the two vessels as they rose and fell out of synch. Eventually he made the leap across with a helping hand from the ship's crew.

'Where's the casualty?'

'Down below. He fell on deck and hurt his shoulder. He's in agony.'

'I'll take a look, but we'll have to get him up here. The coastguard's on the way to do a medevac to the mainland.'

The initial assessment made it apparent he was dealing with a dislocated shoulder. Alasdair administered some pain-relieving medical gas and bandaged up the shoulder to keep the arm stable until the patient got to hospital.

'They can give you stronger pain relief in A&E before they try to manipulate that shoulder back in place,' he reassured the man.

It wasn't long before the lights and whirring sounds in the air were followed by the chopper blades stirring up the water as the coastguard arrived on the scene.

'They're going to lower a ladder and harness you to a crew member,' he shouted to the injured man against the noise as they battled the wind generated by the helicopter.

He relayed his diagnosis and treatment before the casualty was winched up into the air and flown off to the mainland. Once again they were plunged into darkness and Alasdair had to choose his steps carefully back onto the lifeboat.

It was a long journey towing the ship behind them, hampered by the line snapping several times as the weather fought against their progress. By the time they made it back to the boathouse the sun was beginning to peek through the gloom. The adrenaline rush had worn off and that familiar weariness began to settle back into his bones.

As the boat was winched into storage he was fantasising about a hot bath, a cooked breakfast and a few hours' sleep. They still had to wash the boat down to get rid of the salt water, restock and refuel so they were ready for the next shout.

He got more than he bargained for when he did finally stumble into the crew room.

'Shona?'

She was curled up in his chair, huddled under her coat, looking like a dormouse hibernating for the winter.

When she didn't stir, he reached out and brushed the curtain of hair away from her face. She seemed so peaceful. A world away from everything he'd just been through. It was a shame to wake her but the others wouldn't be far behind him and he knew she'd be embarrassed for them to see her here.

'Shona,' he whispered into her ear.

A sleepy smile spread across her face and his weary body was suddenly invigorated again. She took her time stretching out her limbs as she came round. When she opened her eyes and saw him, she blinked furiously before sitting up straight.

'Alasdair. I was waiting for you.'

'I can see that.' He couldn't help but smile at the thought.

'I came to give you your credit card back.' She reached for her bag and began rummaging inside.

'It could've waited,' he said gently. 'I didn't think you were going to go on a spending spree with it.'

'It's stupid; I thought I'd make you a hot drink for coming back. I didn't realise you would be out there so long. I guess I fell asleep.'

'I guess you did. I appreciate the gesture but yeah, it was a long night. We had a medevac and a stricken ship to get ashore. Sometimes it's nothing more than a kid going out too far on an inflatable dinghy. Tonight was a doozy.'

'I'm sure you're exhausted. I'll let you get

home.' She gathered up her coat and pulled on the black boots which were propped up against the chair.

'You know what it's like after the drama of a late shift. I'm too wired to sleep yet. Let me shout you breakfast since I had to bail on dinner.' All traces of tiredness had disappeared since he'd found her waiting for him like an anxious partner. Wishful thinking on his part, but it was nice to imagine she cared enough to worry. He was sure no one else did.

Shona checked the time. 'Isn't it a little early?'

'I know a place,' he said, leading her out of the boathouse before anyone spotted them together. This was an opportunity to impress her he might not get again, and he was going to make the most of it. Even if it did entail misleading her slightly and putting off a trivial thing such as sleep to spend time with the first woman to ever hold his heart.

CHAPTER FOUR

'I ASSUMED YOU meant a café with unusual opening hours or a bakery that sold croissants fresh out of the oven.' Shona hesitated by the door as Alasdair unlocked it.

'Trust me, this will be much better.'

She hoped he was still talking about food as he led her into the house, her belly rumbling.

'I take it this is your place?' The huge glass-fronted house on the hill was a definite upgrade from the shabby shack he'd grown up in. It was no surprise the subsequent tenants had refurbished it since, but it wasn't a patch on this beautiful, airy home he was living in now.

'It's handy for work.' He left her gazing out of the living room window to start prepping in the kitchen area.

'I can see that.' The boathouse was visible at the bottom of the hill, a mere five-minute walk away. Something he'd clearly taken into account when signing the lease. From last night's sudden disappearance and the nature of his job, a quick response time was the difference between life and death. She shuddered thinking about what he put himself through out there and the unpredictability of his life. It was everything that scared her.

'Sweet or savoury?' he asked as he began whisking eggs and milk in a bowl.

'Excuse me?' She moved over to the counter to investigate what he was doing. Her stomach might have made the decision on her behalf to agree to breakfast but her head would decide if his cooking was worth taking a risk.

'I'm making French toast. Sweet or savoury?' He coated slices of bread in the mixture whilst putting some strips of bacon into a sizzling pan.

'Um…both?' She was craving something sweet to give her a boost of energy after a night wedged into an armchair, but the smell of bacon was irresistible.

'Done. If you could get some plates out, I'll make some fruit salad so we can pretend it's healthy.'

'This is my kind of breakfast.' She searched his surprisingly well-organised cupboards for plates and cutlery. Poured two glasses of the fresh orange juice she found in the fridge, then took her seat on a high stool to watch him cook. There was a sense of having missed a significant step between dinner and breakfast. A thought she didn't need to dwell on too long for her own sanity. It seemed that finding out the truth about their 'break-up' had left her more susceptible to his obvious charms. She no longer had a grudge to bear and a reason to push him away. Yet her sense of self-preservation deemed it necessary.

'I aim to please.'

Alasdair's promise to deliver pleasure sent little tingles zipping here, there and everywhere over Shona's entire body. The very reason she shouldn't be letting her mind wander beyond the kitchen.

He finally presented her with a plate of golden-brown French toast, dusted with cinnamon and sugar with a side of bacon. The fruit salad, a mixture of berries and sliced citrus, arrived in a ramekin dish. Her mouth was watering before the first bite.

'I didn't know you could cook.' The sweet, fluffy eggy bread was so light she couldn't get enough of it.

Alasdair washed his down with a mouthful of orange juice.

'I had to learn. Dad could barely microwave a plate of beans. We never had much in the cupboards, so I had to get creative at times. Although some of those concoctions are best left in the past.' A shudder racked through him and Shona thanked her lucky stars she'd had a more stable upbringing. Where she'd taken basic things like unconditional love and homecooked meals for granted. At that age she hadn't understood how his living conditions could have impacted on the rest of his life. It was a credit to Alasdair alone what he'd achieved in spite of his neglectful parents. Thinking of that young boy raiding the empty cupboards yanked on her heartstrings until it physically hurt.

'This is amazing. You can cook me breakfast any time.'

Alasdair snorted as he drank his juice, starting a coughing fit. 'That's very forward of you but I like a progressive woman. We can have a sleepover whenever you like.'

She tutted and tried to gloss over the accidental innuendo. 'You know what I meant.'

'Yeah, but I'd forgotten how easily I could make you blush.'

Unfortunately, she hadn't. He'd only ever had to walk into the room to make her temperature rise, never mind making lewd suggestions to her.

'As I remember it was a distraction technique you used to stop me from asking personal questions.' He'd often teased her when she'd tried to make any serious conversation. Now she knew why. He'd been embarrassed about things at home. Perhaps if anyone had taken the time or interest to investigate what was going on in the background he would have been taken into care. There was no way of knowing if that would have made things any better for him.

'I have nothing to hide now. I'm an open book if you fancy flicking through the pages.'

It was too good an opportunity to turn down.

'Okay. I'll take a peek inside. Why did you come back to the island?'

'I could ask you the same thing.'

'You could but I'm not obliged to answer.' The last thing she wanted was for Alasdair to start treating her with kid gloves when he discovered she was a widow. It was kind of nice to get back to their bantering best like old times. When she'd thought he was an arrogant rebel without a clue and he'd seen her as a spoilt brat. Before he'd made her blush with a simple word or a look. In a time before they'd begun hanging out together, gradually getting closer and coming to know one another. Until she'd believed she was in love for the first and last time.

How naïve she'd been.

'Bad break-up.' The succinct answer brought her back into the room. 'I also thought it was time to make amends with my old man.'

'Oh?' That want to understand him better made her keen to find out more about both of his reasons. Especially how he could forgive someone who'd caused him so much pain.

'Yeah. Despite everything, he's the only family I've got. He's in a nursing home now and it's still difficult but for different reasons. Half of the time he doesn't know who I am and for the other half he doesn't seem to care.'

'Yet you still visit?' The old Alasdair couldn't wait to get away from his father and Shona was beginning to believe his insistence that he was a different person from the boy she'd once known. He was certainly a more forgiving person than she'd been towards him.

'It's not easy. Especially when I'm bombarded with insults for the duration of every visit, but family's family.'

She was jolted back to the audible memories of what he'd been subjected to by his parent in his youth and couldn't help but empathise. 'If you ever need back-up support, just give me a shout. I've got plenty of experience dealing with crotchety patients. Though I don't know why you would give him a second chance after everything he did or said to you.'

He shrugged. 'Life's too short to hold grudges, don't you think?'

'I'm still working on that one.' She stabbed the last piece of bread with her fork, wishing she was able to hold on to the bad memories and keep her crumbling defences in place.

'Let it go, Shona. You'll be all the happier for it.' In one swift movement he leaned over and snatched the last of her breakfast with his mouth.

'I can't believe you just did that.' The brazen theft made her chuckle.

'Old habits die hard,' he said with a wink, sending her temperature rocketing again.

'I suppose I should get home and put my head down for a while before my next shift.' Things were getting too cosy, much too familiar for her to be comfortable with, and she was going to have a hell of a time trying to explain all this to Chrissie.

'Me too. That offer of a sleepover still stands...' It was difficult to know if he was serious or messing with her again.

Either way she had to get out of here quick. Breakfast with Alasdair, trading innuendoes and friendly banter, was the opposite of what she'd expected. Apparently, she was useless at holding a grudge too.

Alasdair saw her out to the front door when she declined the tempting invitation.

'Thanks for breakfast. It was lovely and unexpected.'

'No problem. I'm glad I can still surprise you.

In a good way.' He leaned casually in the doorway as she walked out into the morning haze.

Since she was wearing yesterday's clothes and her make-up was likely smudged from sleep, she was aware what this looked like. She should have been embarrassed but she was grateful for a lot of things.

On tiptoe, she reached up and kissed him on the cheek. 'I'm glad you're safe.'

It wasn't until she'd said it that she realised how anxious she'd been waiting for him to come home last night. She could have walked away at any point but she'd chosen to stay and spend time with him.

Apparently, her little crush had flared dangerously back to life.

Not helped when he shouted after her, 'Remember, you're welcome in my bed any time.'

'You dirty stop-out!' Chrissie greeted her when she walked into the living room.

'It's not what you think.' Shona dropped into the nearest chair, too tired to explain what had, or hadn't, happened with Alasdair when she was at a loss to explain it to herself.

'Then spill, because my imagination has been running riot all night.' Chrissie threw herself into the chair beside her, poised to hear the tale.

'In which case I hate to disappoint you. The

evening really wasn't that exciting.' At least not in the way her sister was thinking. For Shona, the events had left her tons to process. His explanation and apology, the insight into his upbringing, relationship break-up and reason for coming back was a lot to cover over one meal. Two, if she counted breakfast. Which she did when that was what had sent her into a tailspin.

The easy conversation as they'd eaten breakfast had been as disturbing as the innuendo and her physical reaction to something as small as kissing him on the cheek. Coming back into contact with Alasdair was every bit as damaging to her wellbeing as she'd imagined but for an altogether different reason.

For the whole of her married life she'd never been interested in another man. She'd settled for everything she'd had with Iain. One day getting to know Mr Murray again and she remembered she hadn't taken a vow of chastity at any point in time. There were urges and feelings she'd forgotten about and wasn't entirely sure how to handle. Especially when the man they were targeting had hurt her so badly in the past.

'I don't care, I want all the details. It has to be more interesting than getting two toddlers ready for the day.'

'We had scallops... Alasdair ordered some wine...'

'Okay, okay. Maybe not all the details. I don't need to know the contents of the entire menu. I mean, did you confront him about the past? Did you bury the hatchet? And yes, that is a euphemism.' Chrissie's interest was entirely based on her own lack of a love life. She'd told Shona so that time she'd been trying to get her to join a dating app.

'If I can't do it, I want to hear about it,' had been her disturbing reasoning. However, Shona had insisted she was still in her mourning period and not in the right frame of mind to do anything of the sort. Now she was beginning to doubt herself.

'You're obsessed,' she laughed and swatted her sister's knee.

'It's like being on a diet. A sex diet. You crave what you can't have.'

'Who says you can't have it? You're single and gorgeous. Who wouldn't want to hook up with you?'

'How about every man I've ever met? Hello. Single mum of twins. Does that say fun times to you? Anyway, I'm too tired to do anything past seven o'clock. I'd be face down in the appetiser snoring and not making for stimulating company.'

'I'm sure there's someone out there waiting for you.'

'I wish he'd get a move on. I'm not getting any younger. Now, stop getting me side-tracked. What happened between you two last night?'

'He got called out halfway through dinner.'

'No. Then where've you been all this time?'

'I stopped by the boathouse and fell asleep waiting for him to come back.'

'Oh. That's so sweet and boring.'

'I told you. No scandal here.' Seeing the look of disappointment flash across Chrissie's face, Shona decided to give her one juicy morsel of gossip.

'He did invite me back to his place for breakfast.'

'I hope that was his really unsubtle way of asking you for a bunk-up.'

'We had French toast and a nice chat.'

'Hmm. So why do you seem so shifty? I see that rising colour in your cheeks and you can't look me in the eye. There's something more, isn't there?' She was on the edge of her seat now, caught up in the intrigue and possible romance she'd conjured in her head.

'I made a stupid comment about him cooking breakfast for me any time and he said I was welcome to a sleepover whenever I fancied.' The implications of which were making her blink wide-eyed like an innocent schoolgirl all over again.

Chrissie bounced out of her chair with a squeal and grabbed Shona's hands. 'What an offer! Tell me you said yes.' Her eyes were bugging out with excitement and Shona hated to spoil the moment with the truth.

She shook her head. 'That's never going to happen. I've only just forgiven him for something he did fifteen years ago. I'm not about to jump into bed with him.'

'You're not teenagers now. There's no need to worry about your reputation or being judged. In fact, I'll judge you more for not sleeping with the most gorgeous, most eligible man on the island.'

'I'm not that shallow. I don't do one-night stands or casual flings, and he is definitely not the kind of man I want to get into a relationship with either.' If she'd learned one thing last night, it was how dangerous and unsuited to her Alasdair's world could be. He was the very definition of a risky investment when it came to her emotions.

'Pity.' Chrissie pouted. 'I guess I'll have to make do with my emergency supply of raunchy novels to keep me warm during these next cold months.'

Shona stuck her fingers in her ears. 'I don't want to hear this. Now, if we're finished discussing Alasdair Murray, I need to get some sleep before work.'

'You're such a bore,' Chrissie shot after her as she headed upstairs to her room. Away from all thoughts of her night with Alasdair and the morning after.

Shona had only managed a few hours' sleep and restless ones at that. The peace she had sought eluded her as dreams of Alasdair in danger out at sea kept her tossing and turning. Along with images of what they could have been doing all morning.

Eventually she gave up, threw the bed covers off with a curse and attempted to shower away all traces of the previous evening. A quick change of clothes and she was ready to start the day over. Pretend breakfast with Alasdair had never happened.

'Hey. I wasn't expecting to see you up yet. Did we make too much noise?'

As Shona walked into the kitchen Chrissie and the girls were whipping up a batch of cupcakes and chaos. They were fighting over who got to lick the wooden spoon and the smoke alarm was going off as something turned to charcoal in the oven. Chrissie climbed up onto a chair to waft a tea towel in front of the smoke detector.

'No. I just had trouble getting to sleep.' Her time here had been raucous and wonderful. The noise no longer bothered her. If anything, it was a pleasant reminder she wasn't on her own. She had family.

'I think I'll take a walk and clear my head.' One glance around the kitchen, taking in the flour-covered floor, and the broken eggshells spilling the last of their contents down the cupboard doors, and Shona just wanted a little breathing space to herself.

The afternoon sun was bright but when she exhaled her breath hung in the air like wisps of white clouds. She pulled her scarf up over her cold nose and dug her gloved hands deep into her pockets. In the city the roads would have been jammed with traffic and angry drivers who couldn't get where they wanted to be quickly enough. The streets would be thronged with busy shoppers, arms laden with purchases for the upcoming holidays, the smell of petrol hanging in the air along with the various aromas from nearby food outlets.

She thought she'd miss city life, having lived in Edinburgh for so long, but she was enjoying the peace and sense of solitude. There'd been a skiff of snow at some point, but it lay undisturbed on the ground, so she felt like the first person on the moon, leaving her mark. The sound of the sea accompanied her walk, reminding her she had a love-hate relationship with it. When they'd been young, she and Chrissie had always played down on the beach, building sandcastles and splashing in the waves. It had been her go-to place when she needed space to think. Something she had later had in common with Alasdair. It was the place where they'd sat together to forget their troubles.

Unfortunately, it was also where she'd lost her father in a storm. So far from home and safety.

She shivered looking out at the sea, the angry grey waves displaying its strength. Since then she had stopped swimming out there, but a walk along the edge of the shore let her get lost in the rhythm of the tide and breathe in the invigorating salty air.

When the wind began to stymie her progress along the beach, she sought shelter in a grassy alcove among the dunes. She sat down on the sand and hugged her knees, wondering what Alasdair was doing and rendering the whole trip a futile exercise. Hopefully he was sleeping or working in the boathouse. Somewhere safe.

From her haven she watched the gulls nose-diving for their dinner in the distance, the dog walkers getting trailed along the beach by their canine charges and the sun gradually being blocked out by heavy storm clouds.

She knew she couldn't sit here for ever. Although she no longer had a husband to go home to, she had other responsibilities. Her life hadn't ended simply because she was no longer part of a couple. This was her new chapter.

She got up and dusted the sand from her jeans. Directly in her eyeline she could see one of the dog walkers who'd passed by earlier. Only now he was carrying a lead without his dog attached. He was standing at the water's edge yelling out to sea.

Shona moved further down the beach and finally caught sight of the dog out in the water. The great lump of golden fur was little more than a dot in the distance.

To her horror the owner dropped the lead on the sand, kicked off his shoes and shed his jacket. His intentions were clear.

'No! Stop!' she yelled too late as he launched himself into the surf after his beloved pet, which was clearly in trouble.

Shona knew the sea would be too wild, too cold that far out on a day like today for anyone to come out unscathed. Even if he was an excellent swimmer, goodness knew how he'd manage to bring the dog back with him. That was if his limbs were still working after being immersed in the icy water. It didn't take long for hypothermia to set in or the shock from the cold to disorient a person either. Sure enough, the man began to slow as he reached the dog, then he was doing nothing more than treading water and signalling for help.

When working in A&E she knew how to respond in a crisis because she had a wealth of medical knowledge and access to the best facilities and treatment. Here, she was pacing the shoreline, seemingly powerless to prevent a tragedy.

There was one person who could help in this situation. She pulled out her phone, relieved Alasdair had insisted she take his number in case she ever needed him. Boy, did she need him now.

The wait for him to answer was interminable. Finally, a drowsy Alasdair whispered a husky, 'Hello.'

'Alasdair? It's Shona. I'm on the beach. There was a dog…it swam too far from shore…the owner went in… I need your help.' It took everything in her to admit that to him. This past year she'd soldiered on through everything, stayed strong because she'd had to. For once there was someone else who could share the burden.

She heard the rustling sheets and pictured him getting out of bed to pull on his clothes.

'I'll get the boat launched but I need you to call the coastguard to log the call.'

'Okay.'

Just before he hung up, he added, 'Everything's going to be all right.'

Shona appreciated the reassurance. He knew what he was doing and was confident about it. Once she'd informed the coastguard of the incident and location, all she could do was wait. Every now and then she shouted against the wind, hoping the man in trouble could hear that help was on its way.

Thoughts of her father and his last moments came flooding to mind. How he must have suffered out there, cold and alone, not knowing if someone would save him. They hadn't. By the time someone found him it had been too late.

When the lifeboat finally came into view, tears were streaming down her face and stinging her cheeks in the cold. Her toes were numb. But she wouldn't move until she knew everyone out there was all right.

She could make out Alasdair at the helm, head and broad shoulders above his crew mates, and her heart lurched along with the boat in the churning waves. They came alongside the struggling pair in the water and the Alasdair-shaped figure hauled the dog into the boat first, followed by his two-legged friend.

A support vehicle roared across the sand and Shona realised the crew were coming ashore. Her heart was hammering in fear and relief as they came closer into view. She'd done the right thing enlisting Alasdair's help, but had essentially put him in danger. It was his job, but this was an up-close viewing of what that entailed. Even attending what was likely a low-level incident for the crew, it was obvious the weather and the conditions were changeable and a serious risk to all involved. It certainly wasn't the type of work which guaranteed you'd come home at five o'clock every night, if at all. Certainly not the life of someone she'd ever want to get close to.

Alasdair was the first to jump out of the dinghy, splashing through the shallows to pull the others ashore. Closely followed by the bedraggled retriever, which bounded out and headed straight for Shona.

Tail wagging, tongue lolling, he jumped up and nearly knocked her off her feet with his huge wet paws. There was no sign of trauma from his experience as he slobbered all over her face.

'Dave, get down,' the dog's owner scolded with the little energy he probably had left after his ordeal. Alasdair was helping him out of the boat, a blanket wrapped around his shivering shoulders.

'He's fine. I'm just glad everyone's okay.' She looked up from ruffling 'Dave' behind the ears to catch Alasdair's eye. His brief smile before he turned his attention back to Dave's owner told her he appreciated her concern.

He sat the human casualty down in the back of the four-by-four to let him catch his breath. The driver reached out with a flask and poured a cup of hot tea for the man they'd just picked up.

He clung on to it like a lifeline, body shaking and teeth chattering. 'I can't thank you enough. When I saw Dave struggling to stay afloat, I just jumped in without thinking.'

'It happens a lot, but next time call us before you think of going in yourself. Okay?' Alasdair went easy on him, probably hoping the experience had been lesson enough.

Shona approached the support vehicle so he could be reunited with Dave.

'Daft mutt. You nearly got us both killed.' He buried his face in the dog's wet fur to hide his tears and she had to swallow hers before attempting to speak.

'Dave seems fine, but you should probably go and get checked over at the hospital.' Her colleagues would be there to assist should he suffer any after-effects of his ordeal.

'I'm fine. Tired and cold, but I only live across the road. A hot bath and a wee dram of whisky are all I need. Thank you, everyone.'

'We'll give you a lift home, but Shona's right, any problems at all and you should go and get checked over.' Alasdair reiterated her worries, but she couldn't blame the man for simply wanting to get home and get dry. She was starting to shiver herself and she hadn't been swimming in her clothes.

'You should get home too. You're freezing.' Alasdair had noticed and began rubbing his hands up and down her arms to generate some heat. So much she was ready to burst into flames. She might as well not have been wearing three layers of her winter wardrobe when she swore she could feel his very fingers on her skin.

'Yes, I probably should.' Another shudder which had nothing to do with the weather took over her body. To a different woman it wouldn't be a problem to have a handsome, hard-working man touching her and bringing every inch of her to attention. These past few days Alasdair had developed a way of making her forget she was a widow and that they had the kind of history which should make her wary. Perhaps she needed a little detox. Some space to remember who they both were at heart.

CHAPTER FIVE

'ARE YOU ON overtime or something? It seems as though you're never away from this place lately. Not that I'm complaining.' Gerry, the winchman on the crew, ripped off a hunk of homemade bread and dipped it into the bowl of hearty broth Alasdair had set before him.

'I was using up the contents of my fridge and thought you guys could do with something a little more nutritious than burgers.' Alasdair was supposed to be taking it easy at home after a late-night mayday call to rescue a fishing boat which had hit rocks and was taking in water. They'd managed to save the lone fisherman and his vessel, but the incident had gone on into the early hours of the morning.

He had cover for the day, but he seemed to be having difficulty switching off his brain to manage time off to relax. After completing his household chores and doing some cooking, he figured he may as well be restless in company.

So far the guys dropping into the boathouse seemed appreciative of his efforts.

'You'll make someone a good wife,' Gerry said with a grin, before slurping up some more of the soup.

The joke was an ongoing one with the guys at the boathouse, most of whom were married with children. There had been numerous attempts to set him up with their wives' friends and relations, without success. Alasdair had been content on his own for quite some time. In the years since coming back to Braelin he'd only had one woman stay for breakfast. Shona.

He'd teased her about sleeping over, but he'd merely succeeded in torturing himself with the idea, forgetting that they'd only just managed to get back on speaking terms. He supposed he'd had her on something of a pedestal since they'd been kids. She was the cute girl next door with the loving family and the kind heart. Much too good for the likes of him, then. He'd kept that idealised version of her in his head all this time. Yet he'd wanted to spend that time with her in his kitchen, and elsewhere, when she'd clearly been concerned for his wellbeing.

He couldn't remember the last time he'd had someone wait up for him, had a woman to come back to. No matter that she'd deny it if he confronted her about it, she cared. He'd seen it in her eyes that day on the beach too and it tugged at something deep inside him. A longing for that which had been missing from his life too long. Companionship. Love. Family.

Natasha had made him fearful to want those things again and hardened his heart against the possibility. He'd accepted he was destined to be on his own like his father. They finally had something in common. They were on their own, burned by love and rejection.

Alasdair knew when it had come out about Natasha getting rid of the baby he'd never trust easily again. More than that, he didn't think he could invest as heavily again in a relationship, or a future with someone else. Natasha had broken more than his heart. She'd destroyed the image of his perfect family he'd had in his head since the day she showed him the positive pregnancy test. No, a baby hadn't been something they'd planned, but the idea of becoming a father had meant the world to him. Having that stolen from him without even having a conversation about it had left him grieving for the child who would never be his. It turned out it was just *his* baby she hadn't wanted. He'd since found out she was married with two children. That revelation had felt like another bereavement and knocked him for six again. Every time his heart and soul were ground into finer and finer dust, he knew he couldn't take much more. It became harder to pick himself up and carry on. That was when he'd made the decision to put relationships on the back burner. Instead, he'd concentrated on his career and the only family he'd ever had. His father.

Seeing Shona again made him think about happier times in his past. He was discovering the pleasure of getting to know her again, and himself. She'd set off that spark inside him once more, a zest for fun he'd believed snuffed out by betrayal and grief. Something he hadn't found on the island again until she'd arrived. He was beginning to wonder if his life here was almost as fake as the one he'd had with his ex. Had he been pretending that his job was enough to fulfil him when a part of him still longed to be that loved-up teenage boy?

He went to work, participated in the community where he could and supported his father, but really he had no personal life beyond that. This was the first time since moving home he had thought about what it might be like to have someone at home with him. To share breakfast with and more. He'd had a taste of it with Shona, teasing her and enjoying her company. While he didn't think either of them were in the right headspace for anything more, he enjoyed spending time with her.

The Winter Wonderland was the perfect excuse to keep seeing her. At least now he had something to look forward to, unlike the visits to see his father that he felt duty-bound to make but which took a mental toll on him every time. He wondered if Shona's presence would provide the antidote to the poison often spewed at him when he stopped by the nursing home. She'd volunteered to go with him when he'd told her what he faced. At first, he'd taken it for nothing more than lip service, a polite gesture of support. However, her apparent concern for him on his call-out was making him think differently. Whilst he didn't want to subject her unnecessarily to his father's temper or vitriol, it would be nice to have someone with him.

An idea began to form in his head, snowballing into a new mission. Operation Dress Rehearsal would take the pressure off them both, providing an excuse for them to be together and at the same time accepting Shona's offer of support. All he had to do was get into character and hopefully he could deflect anything his father had to throw at him.

The time always seemed to fly during a busy shift but today Shona thought it wasn't going quickly enough. When Alasdair had called to say they had their first official engagement she was filled with a mixture of excitement and dread. She'd almost got used to that fluttering in her belly any time she heard his voice or saw his face, but the idea of having to put on a performance alongside him detracted from any idea of having a good time. It reminded her too much of her marriage. Playing a part to fool those around them. On the surface she'd been happy, but dig a little deeper and she'd been full of regret about giving up on the idea of passionate love just to wrap her tender heart up in cotton wool. She wondered if coming back here and getting to know her old self again meant opening herself up to the idea of love once more. A scary thought.

'What exciting plans have you got for tonight, Shona? I'm doing nothing except putting my feet up and watching the telly.' Joanna, one of her nursing colleagues, was counting down to the end of the shift along with her.

'I, um, I'm visiting the nursing home later. It's my first engagement as Chief Elf.' It sounded ridiculous and it was, when a grown woman was expected to dress up and throw pixie dust about. She hoped she could do the job justice.

Joanna giggled. 'I wish I could be there to see it.'

'Oh, I'm sure you will at some point. My diary is going to be very full with public appearances leading up to Christmas.' Her stomach tightened at the very thought. Drawing attention to herself was the opposite of how she'd been living her life here so far. When people saw her with Alasdair they'd be asking even more questions about the man she'd left the island to marry and what had happened to him.

'I'm sure you'll be amazing. You're great with the patients here, young and old.' Joanna gave her a hug, perhaps sensing her trepidation over her upcoming appointment. Shona appreciated the compliment and the confidence shown in her by one of the department's longest-serving staff members. She loved her job taking care of people, comforting and reassuring the sick and injured. It gave her a real sense of purpose and achievement. Perhaps that was the way she should look at her new role too. Providing a service to the community rather than an exercise in public exposure.

She was about to go and get her things as home time crept up on the clock when a flash of red caught her eye at the door.

'Ho, ho, ho. Merry Christmas!'

All heads in the waiting room turned to watch the figure at the entrance. It took a moment for Shona to register who it was behind the bushy white beard and cheery red suit.

'Alasdair?'

'Now, now, don't go giving away my identity,' he whispered as he took her arm and spun her away from the watching crowd.

'What are you doing here? I thought we were meeting later?' When she'd had some time to prepare herself mentally for spending the evening with him and dressing up to entertain the elderly residents at the home. She knew why he'd chosen that particular place to start spreading their Christmas joy. Where she was afraid these characters they'd be playing would expose her, leave her vulnerable, Alasdair was hiding behind his portly façade. If he visited the home as his alter ego, he could avoid the reality of the situation with his father for one afternoon at least. She didn't blame him. Except for continuing to turn her world upside down.

'If we go now, it means we have the rest of the evening to ourselves.'

'Now? I can't go like this. I've just finished work.' Even the greatest actor couldn't convince a room full of adults that Santa's elf dressed in scrubs in her downtime.

'Not a problem. I thought you could change here before we go.' He swung the red velvet sack down from over his shoulder and pulled the gold drawstring loose, revealing the contents.

Shona put her hand inside and pulled out her costume. 'You've got to be kidding me.'

She knew Alasdair was hiding a wide smile behind his full white beard.

'You have to look the part.'

'Of what? A giant frog?' She was confronted by a sea of emerald-green velvet. A tunic and knickerbockers, teamed with green-and-white stripy stockings for good measure, for her to don.

St Nick stuck his hand into the sack and pulled out a matching hat with white fur trim, and pointy felt ears to complete the look. 'I'll wait while you change.'

The heavy cloak of impending doom which usually settled around Alasdair's shoulders when he pulled up outside the care home was missing today. His Chief Elf looked anxious, but he was hoping once they got into the spirit of Christmas she'd relax into her character.

'You look great.' He watched as she added rosy circles to her cheeks and some glitter on her face. It would probably be inappropriate to tell her what fabulous legs she had when she was probably freezing in those knee-high stockings.

'Wish I could say the same. That outfit does nothing for you,' she said with a grin.

Alasdair laughed as his fake belly got wedged

under the steering wheel when he tried to get out of his seat.

'It's just as well I'm not here to find myself a girlfriend in that case. Now, I've phoned ahead, and the staff have gathered the residents in the rec room.' He refilled Santa's sack with the small gifts he had stashed in the boot of his car.

'For what? You haven't told me what we're supposed to be doing other than dressing up. That might be enough for kids keen to get their photograph taken with Santa Claus, but I'm not sure that's going to be entertaining for the older community.' Shona adjusted her elf ears and Alasdair again had to refrain from telling her how adorable she looked. She sounded anxious about doing this and he had no desire to make her any more self-conscious than she was already.

'It's nothing too taxing, don't worry. We're just going to hand out a few presents and I'll play some Christmas tunes on my phone to make it a bit more festive. Just a bit of fun to brighten their day.' His dad would sneer at any attempt to have 'fun', especially if it involved his son dressing up in a ridiculous outfit, but Alasdair thought this was a less humiliating way for his father to berate him. At least he'd have a reason to do it today.

'I don't sing,' Shona warned him, before they reached the door.

'That's fine. I told you, I've got the music covered.' He waved his phone at her.

Christmas was supposed to be a joyous time, but, apart from the requisite present handing-over to his father, the last few had been lonely. He'd had a few offers to spend the day with the crew and their families but would never impose on people that way. The invitations were issued out of pity and politeness. If he was going to spend Christmas with anyone it would be nice if it was with someone who actually wanted to be with him. It might never happen, but given the choice he'd enjoy opening presents and tucking into a turkey dinner with someone like Shona. Who was he kidding? Not someone like her, just her. If she didn't bristle him so damned much when he was near.

At least the care home staff were happy to see him as he announced his arrival. 'Ho, ho, ho. Merry Christmas! I hear there are some good boys and girls here at Golden Years who deserve a little treat.'

'I think you're it.' The care assistant in Reception tapped her pen against her teeth and eyed him hungrily as though he were wearing something a lot sexier than a fat suit.

Alasdair hadn't seen her here before and

wasn't prepared for the attention. 'I...er...we... er...'

He'd had some interest from the opposite sex over the years and had always managed to deflect it without a fuss. It was the fact it was happening in front of Shona which had thrown him.

'What he's trying to stutter is that they're waiting for us in the rec room if it wouldn't be too much trouble for you to show us the way.' Shona stepped up to the desk, providing a much-needed barrier between him and the flirtatious member of staff, whilst he tried to compose himself.

Gayle, according to the name badge, reluctantly peeled herself away from the desk, glaring at Shona as she did so.

'Totally inappropriate,' his disgruntled elf companion seethed as they made their way down the brightly lit hallway, following the sounds of loud chatter and the blare of a television at full volume.

Alasdair hoped she couldn't see him smiling beneath his beard. It would only rile her more. He, on the other hand, was on cloud nine to see her bothered by someone paying him some attention. It meant there were feelings there of some description. Even if she was driven by irritation, it was preferable to indifference. Besides, he'd have to be made of stone if he weren't slightly turned on by two attractive women sizing each other up on either side of him as though they were about to wrestle over him.

For a moment he'd let his imagination get the better of him.

'Stay here.' Gayle wasn't so accommodating now Shona appeared to have marked her territory, and Alasdair wasn't complaining on either account.

They stayed outside the double doors as one of the friendlier, less predatory members of staff was notified of their imminent arrival. She promptly switched off the television and within moments the group of residents was engaged in an enthusiastic rendition of a popular Christmas song.

'I think that's our cue.' He grinned at Gayle, then drank in Shona's scowl. His unhappy little elf was nearly as green as her outfit and it only made Alasdair want to ham it up even more. He found he wanted to make her jealous, to realise she still liked him. Goodness knew why when he knew she was only with him because she was contractually obliged to be. It wasn't going to boost his ego any to set his cap at someone else who didn't really want to spend time with him. That was just asking for more heartache on top of an ex who'd rejected a life with him for someone 'better'.

Thankfully, for those looking forward to his presence, Shona was professional, so the second the doors opened she was smiling away and captivating the room. He saw the elderly gents' mouths drop open when she walked in and karma paid him an unwelcome visit. It wasn't funny to have anyone stare at her with undisguised admiration. Yet it had been his idea to dress her up and parade her around the island with him. He was simply going to have to suck it up for the rest of December and accept the rest of the male population wasn't immune to her charms. She was no longer his to be territorial over. He'd given up that right when he'd realised he'd never be good enough for her the first time around.

Alasdair waved to the assembled crowd, scanning the room to find his father. He hadn't given him any warning about his unorthodox appearance today, but judging by the expression on his face he'd already recognised his son. Arms folded with a scowl ploughed right across his forehead, he was glaring at Alasdair. He ignored him for now, although the nausea was beginning to kick in at having to face him in public.

'Well, Father Christmas, don't we have some gifts to distribute to everyone?' Shona gave him a nudge to get back in the room.

'We sure do, my elfie little friend.'

Clearly still not one hundred per cent on board with her character, she purposefully trod on his foot when she helped him take out some of the presents from the bag. Although her green pixie slippers with bells on didn't make much of an impact on his steel-toe-capped boots.

He started his Christmas playlist of songs whilst they handed out the presents. This visit wasn't technically part of the Winter Wonderland schedule, but he'd suggested it to the care-home manager in the hope it would lift everyone's spirits a little. Now he could see the smiles they'd put on most people's faces he was glad she'd agreed. There were only a few who went home with family for the holidays and even less who had visitors. With the weather as bad as it was at this particular time of year, they didn't really have the option of day trips either. He wanted them to know they weren't forgotten here. They were still part of the community.

'Let's start with Miss Florrie here. You've been a good girl this year.' He gave one of the boxes of his homemade fudge to the lovely lady who always fetched him a cup of tea when he stopped by.

It was tricky to get generic gifts to suit everyone, so he'd made a batch of sweets and bis-

cuits. Alasdair knew most of the residents and
had done his best to tailor to everyone's needs.

'And who have we here?' Shona played along,
looking to him to fill her in on names as they
went around the room.

'This is Angus. Are you sure we don't have
any coal in there?' he teased the ruddy-cheeked
ex-fisherman who still had a twinkle in his eye
and a hearty laugh for the pair.

They alternated responsibility for the gift-
giving, eventually meeting at his father's seat
in the room. Alasdair was immediately lost for
something to say. Unfortunately, his dad wasn't
suffering from a similar affliction.

'You're an embarrassment, Alasdair. It's no
wonder your mother left. Look at the state of
you.'

'It's just a bit of fun for Christmas, Dad.' He
broke character, trying and failing to keep the
smile on his face while he died a little more inside.

'Hey, Mr Murray. It's good to see you.' Shona
stepped in to shake hands and break some of
the tension, but the damage had been done. Now
Alasdair had some idea of how it must have felt
to her when he'd embarrassed her in front of
people with a few sharp words.

'Who's she?' His father barely acknowledged
her, directing his question at Alasdair.

'This is Shona. She used to live next door to us, remember?' Alasdair appealed to whatever tiny bit of decency might be left in him to be kind to her. He'd been dealing with this venom for his whole life, but she'd done nothing to deserve it.

'The Little Princess. Too good for the likes of you. Why are you dressed like an imbecile anyway?' He shoved Alasdair in the stomach, knocking him off balance so he stumbled back.

'Alasdair was nominated to play Santa Claus this year. He's very well respected in the community, Mr Murray.' Shona continued to engage him in civil conversation and, though Alasdair was grateful she was fighting his corner, he knew it was pointless.

'He's a dirty little thief,' his father spat.

The pity he saw in Shona's eyes when she looked at him was worse than the insult. Then she leaned down and spoke directly into his father's ear. 'He's a good man and you should be proud of him.'

She stood up, the smile back on her face. 'Now, who would like to have a dance?'

Most of the hands in the room shot up. Shona took the hand of one elderly volunteer and brought him to his feet.

'I didn't think you did this sort of thing.' Alasdair could have kissed her for breaking the tension and reminding him why he was here today. Especially if it was coming at the expense of her own comfort.

'I said I don't sing. Dancing I can do. Sort of.' Her distraction helped him to try and put his father's comments behind him. She believed in him, not the opinions of his father, and that was enough for now.

Following her lead, Alasdair left his father stewing in his own hatred to escort an eager resident into the middle of the room for a dance. This was why they'd come. To enrich people's lives and enjoy themselves. If his father wasn't willing to accept all that was on offer there was nothing more Alasdair could do. At least Shona had stood up for him and that was more than he could have wished for. A sign she saw more in him than simply someone she had to endure. Perhaps it was about time he had faith in himself too when it came to the opposite sex, he thought, and realised he shouldn't base the rest of his life solely on Natasha's actions. He might be a man worthy of loving after all.

As he spun his dance partner around the floor and watched Shona laughing as she was twirled around until she looked dizzy, he thought it could be time to let go of the past and embrace the future.

CHAPTER SIX

'THANKS FOR DOING THAT. I know I sprang it on you last-minute, but I think everyone really enjoyed themselves.' Alasdair was beginning to look a lot more like himself as he peeled off his beard and removed the padded red suit. As a way of saying thanks the manager had brought them through to the kitchen for some lunch.

Shona took off her hat and ears and made herself as comfortable as she could on the high stool next to Alasdair. 'I think *nearly* everyone enjoyed themselves.'

Mr Murray had been the exception. Determined, it seemed, not to indulge in any festive cheer or extend any kindness towards his son. She bit into her triangle sandwich with gusto, shredding the ham with her teeth. Almost as viciously as that man had treated his son. Alasdair didn't deserve his wrath. He never had. Max Murray was lucky to have someone like Alasdair willing to continue visiting and being there for him, regardless of how truly awful it must be for him. If that was a sample of the abuse he continued to receive, Alasdair deserved a medal for putting up with it. Yes, it was difficult to tell how much of what his father said was part of the disease warping his brain, but he'd always seemed to have a low opinion of Alasdair. Goodness knew why when he was clearly one of the most respected, kindest people on the island.

Today had been his idea to come and cheer the residents up. Not only had he handmade and wrapped the gifts, but he'd also gone out of his way for those with different dietary requirements, making sure he had sugar-free confectionery for the diabetics and gluten-free for those who were intolerant. Something the real Santa Claus might not have taken the care and time to do with his busy schedule.

'Yes, I'm sorry about him.'

It wasn't even necessary to clarify who it was she was talking about.

'It's not your fault. You were amazing.' Shona thought he needed to hear it from someone. She only had her sister, and her nieces, left and she'd be devastated if the only conversation they had involved a constant volley of insults and bad temper. The love and support she'd discovered with her family again was what had got her through the tough times and made her decide to move back.

Alasdair didn't even have someone at home to appreciate him. This year, until she'd moved in with Chrissie, was the only time in her life she'd been on her own. She knew how difficult it was not having someone to talk over your day with and have them reassure you everything would be okay. Her marriage might not have been the most passionate in the world but Iain had been there for her. As far as she could see, Alasdair had no one. There were still shadows of that lonely boy she'd befriended on the beach, but this time around she knew to keep her heart protected at all times.

'I might need that review to keep hold of my new position.' She could tell he was only half joking and it would be a shame if his father's attitude stole away some of his exuberance for the role.

'Why is he so mean to you anyway? I know he's not well now, but he's always been horrible to you.' It seemed to her the misdemeanours Alasdair had been guilty of in his youth had come about out of necessity and long after his father's reign of verbal and physical abuse.

Alasdair shrugged and sighed. 'Because he never wanted me? Because he blames me for my mother running off? Who knows? I stopped questioning that some time ago. I had to so I could get on with my life.'

'I guess so. Whatever it is, it's his problem, not yours.' She reached out in a gesture of support. Now he'd disrobed, his arms were bare in the white T-shirt he'd been wearing under his coat. Her hand connected with his thick forearm. He was warm beneath her touch, reminding her of that summer they'd spent wrapped in each other's arms. The connection started a series of tiny tremors of pleasure within her body. When she looked up from where her hand was resting on him, he was watching her with that same intensity of his seventeen-year-old self. That lustful stare which kept her locked under the blue tractor beam of his eyes. Would it be so bad to find out if they still generated heat together? Only this time of a more adult nature. Slowly, helplessly, she was drawn towards him, her lips parted in anticipation of a kiss.

'Help yourselves to tea, more sandwiches or cake. We had a little buffet before you arrived. I'm sure you're hungry and you deserve it. They had a ball in there.'

The manager bustled into the kitchen with the remnants of the Christmas party for them to share in. Shona's appetite for anything immediately disappeared when she realised she'd come close to falling into her old bad habits.

These days she had more than her school reputation to worry about—her heart, her peace of mind and likely her sanity.

Shona jumped up off her seat, her skull almost colliding with Alasdair's chin in the process. When he saw that she'd bolted from him he sagged back into his seat with a sigh. His frustration echoed hers, but the interruption had saved her from doing something she knew she'd come to regret.

'Let me help you with that.' She moved swiftly to busy her hands with something other than Alasdair, helping to put dirty dishes into the sink and empty rubbish into the bin. His eyes were practically burning a hole into the back of her head. She could feel him watching her, waiting for her to turn around and look at him, but she needed some space away from that almost-kiss.

In the end the room was so tense, the silence between them broken only by the sound of the water sloshing against the plates as she washed them, that the manager turned the radio on. As every year, the airwaves had been ringing with Christmas tunes since November, so it was no surprise when the kitchen filled with the sound of loud, repetitive festive songs she knew word for word. So did Alasdair, apparently, as he sang tunelessly along. It was almost a relief when a breathless staff member ran in.

When she opened the door the sound of an alarm was blaring somewhere down the corridor. Something which might be commonplace here, but the panicked look on the woman's face expressed the seriousness of whatever was going on. 'It's Mr Finlay...'

The manager immediately sprang into action, following the sound of the alarm to one of the rooms. Shona went after her to see if she could do anything, with Alasdair not far behind.

'I don't think he can breathe.' Another staff member was smacking an elderly male on the back, his face almost purple, his hands clutched around his throat.

'He's choking on something.' Shona knew they'd have first-aid experience in the nursing home but instinct kicked in. If they couldn't dislodge whatever was blocking the airways he could die. She took over the back blows, leaning Mr Finlay forward and supporting him with one hand. With the heel of her other hand she began to administer five sharp blows between his shoulder blades. After each one Alasdair checked his mouth to see if any object was visible.

'Nothing. Do you want me to do the chest thrusts?'

It was the next logical step, and one she'd had to perform on a few occasions, but Mr Finlay was almost three times her size. Alasdair might make more impact with his thrusts and now wasn't the time for her to get territorial. He had medical knowledge and experience too.

'Yes. Did someone phone an ambulance yet?' Shona swapped positions with Alasdair, letting him circle the patient's bulk with his arms.

If they couldn't get his airways clear for him to breathe, they'd have to use specialised equipment in the hospital to remove the object. There could be long-lasting brain damage after five-to-ten minutes if there was no oxygen supply.

'Yes.' The manager was watching the drama unfold, letting them control the proceedings, probably because she knew it was in her resident's best interests.

Alasdair placed one fist against the man's breastbone, grasped it with his other and delivered an inward, upward thrust. Shona checked the mouth for any visible sign of the object and shook her head. They repeated the process another four times. On the very last attempt Mr Finlay emitted a small gasping sound and something hard and round popped out onto the floor.

The manager inspected it while Mr Finlay fought to get as much air as he could back in his lungs.

'John, what have I told you about eating boiled sweets? This isn't the first time you've nearly choked to death on them.' Despite the scolding she was taking his arm and helping him to sit back down on his bed to recover.

Shona knew there was a high rate of choking among the elderly. She'd dealt with a few in her time, inside and outside of the hospital. Due to the aging process, some of the older community found it harder to provide saliva, thus causing problems with chewing and swallowing. Some lacked sufficient teeth to break food down properly, while others had problems with dentures. Various medical conditions such as Parkinson's disease or the after-effects of a stroke also made choking a possibility. That was why trained medical staff on hand and a quick response were vital at times like this.

'That was a close one,' Mr Finlay croaked out, his face a less alarming shade of puce now.

'I think you should probably still let the paramedics check you over when they get here.' Shona didn't think it would do any harm to let them take some readings on his heart rate and blood pressure in case the incident had a delayed effect on him.

'We will.' The matron resumed charge of her rebellious resident and let Shona and Alasdair off the hook. 'Thanks for everything. I'm glad you were both here.'

'I thought my time really had come when you lot came charging in.'

In the excitement it had been easy to forget why they were here and what they looked like. She glanced at Alasdair, half dressed in his baggy Santa trousers and braces, then at her own pixie shoes and stripy stockings. What a sight they must have made to Mr Finlay, running in here and manhandling him. She couldn't help but laugh. Alasdair too.

'We should probably be on our way in case we cause any more disruption.' It was he who made their excuses to leave and Shona was glad of it. She'd been on her feet all day, coming here straight from work. If they didn't go now, who knew what else would crop up, needing their attention?

'Aye, thanks for the tea and sandwiches but we have to get back and feed the reindeer.' She was beginning to see the merits of dressing up and getting out into the community. All drama aside, it had been fun, and she hadn't had a lot of that recently. This time last year she couldn't have imagined dressing up and dancing around, but today had been good. She'd felt part of the community again and that was down to Alasdair. Shona hoped he was top of Santa's nice list this year because he deserved only good things to happen to him.

She knew nothing of his ex, bar two things. The woman hadn't deserved him, and she didn't know what she'd thrown away. As Shona watched him shake hands and kiss the cheeks of the staff before they left she knew deep in her heart he was one of the good guys.

They drove the short distance back to Chrissie's house in silence. Shona was weary in body and soul. Not only for herself.

'It must be hard to listen to that all the time, Alasdair. Why on earth would you come back to subject yourself to that?'

His sigh was amplified by the sound of the engine dying. 'I didn't have anything else in Glasgow. I thought at least here I had family. Even if he does hate me.'

'What on earth happened in Glasgow to make you think this was the best on offer for you?' She understood something of his motives when loneliness had driven her back into the bosom of her family, but at least she'd had something positive to return to.

'You don't want to know.'

'Yes, I do.' If he had no one else to confide in or rely on for support, she was willing to be there again for him. Someone had to be when a person's mental health was at stake. It was impossible not to be affected by a parent's emotional abuse. Even if Alasdair was no longer being physically attacked, his father's behaviour would still leave scars if left untreated.

He drew in a long, slow breath as he braced his hands against the steering wheel. 'My ex, she, um, she got rid of our baby without telling me.'

'Oh, my goodness, Alasdair. I'm so sorry.'

'Yeah, well, it's in the past now but it's a level of betrayal I didn't think I'd ever get over. We'd talked about children, of having the kind of family I never had. I know it was her body, and ultimately her decision, but I was devastated when I found out she'd had an abortion behind my back.' It was no wonder he'd wanted to get as far away as possible. Shona knew something of the difficulties a difference of opinion over children could have on a couple.

'Iain never wanted children. I agreed with him at the time, but there was a yearning inside me that led to resentment as I got older. I was trapped, destined not to be a mother on someone else's say so.'

'Is that why you divorced?' His assumption was understandable when she hadn't been honest about her past or why she'd come back. Perhaps if Iain hadn't got ill a separation would have been likely, but fate had stepped in and taken the decision away from her anyway.

'I'm not divorced. I'm widowed.' There, she'd said it. She waited for the display of pity she hadn't wanted to see in Alasdair's eyes. It wasn't as though she'd been the typical grieving widow. Iain's death had left her numb, unsure of who she was without him in her life but keen to find out.

'You should've said. There was no need to keep it a secret.'

'I haven't really figured out how I feel about it yet. I miss him but we did marry too young. I changed. Given my time over, I'm not sure I would've made the same mistakes.'

'I think we'd all like a chance to go back and do things differently.' In the pressured confines of the car it suddenly seemed as though they had gone back in time. His focus was totally on her, so she knew beyond doubt he meant with her, not his ex.

If this was another way for him to apologise for the things he'd said and done as a teenager, it was working. Those quivers coursing through her entire body would make her forgive him anything. She was trapped, a victim of her own hormones, waiting, anticipating his touch.

The creak of leather sounded the shift in Alasdair's seat as he reached out to her. He caressed her cheek with his hand and leaned in towards her. Shona hesitated at the last second, before their mouths collided, knowing there would be no going back if they kissed. His breath was hot against her lips. She looked up to see his eyes flutter shut and then she was lost.

Their mouths fitted together perfectly the way they always had and her body sighed into the kiss. She'd been waiting for this moment for a long time and was ready to fully embrace it.

Those first few seconds were a tentative reconnection. Lips coming back for more again and again. Then she felt Alasdair's other hand cradling her face and things kicked up a gear. He wanted her. She could tell by the way he began to lose control, his mouth imploring her for more; his tongue tasting, teasing, tangling with hers. It was intoxicating. She let out a little moan of satisfaction and tried to get closer to him, cursing the logistics of trying to make out in a car. Sensing her frustration, and possibly due to his own, Alasdair slid one arm around her and one under her. He lifted her effortlessly onto his lap. An impressive feat on its own. Then she felt the hard, muscular wall of his chest against her palm and swooned.

They were a breathless mass of hormones and entwined limbs, rediscovering their desire for one another, and Shona couldn't get enough of it, or him. It had been too long since anyone had kissed her so passionately or made her feel so damn much. This was more than teenage sweethearts reuniting, this was adult lust, pulsating, wanting, needing to be explored.

His hand was under her tunic, sliding along her bare thigh, and she made no move to stop him. He rounded the curve of her backside, slipping his fingers beneath the flimsy fabric of her knickers. Her breath hitched in her throat as he travelled ever closer to that sensitive place throbbing and ready for his touch. She shifted position to meet him and leaned against the car horn, alerting everyone in the vicinity to what they were up to.

With a sharp curse she scrabbled back into her own seat, leaving Alasdair dazed and wondering what had happened. A glance out of the steamy window confirmed her fear. Chrissie was standing watching from the house, her jaw almost hitting the ground.

'My sister,' she said, attempting to explain the sudden halt to their hot encounter in the front seat of his car.

'Sorry. I didn't mean to embarrass you.' He looked flustered himself and no wonder. They'd both got a little too carried away.

'You didn't. I mean, I don't think either of us saw that coming.'

'No?' His raised eyebrow disputed that.

'Okay, so maybe we had some unfinished

business,' she conceded, thinking not only about their teenage selves but also their breakfast together and the sizzling chemistry she'd walked away from then.

'Had?'

Shona knew her face was scarlet. There was no denying things had come to an unsatisfying ending when her body was still zinging with arousal for the man sitting next to her. 'I don't know what's going on, Alasdair, but it can't happen.'

She could imagine the fun Chrissie was going to have with this one. It was a wonder she wasn't at the car window, waving her pompoms and cheerleading for more.

'I know we've both been through a tough time, Shona, but you know there's something here between us, and I'm not talking about the gear stick.' He laughed at his own lame joke.

'We're too old to be doing this.' She rearranged her clothes and hoped none of the neighbours had witnessed their little display. Being the subject of local gossip was exactly what she'd hoped to avoid.

'Says who? Don't you think we've wasted enough time, Shona?'

'I can't... I've just lost my husband. I'm not ready.' She was so conflicted. Her head was telling her one thing whilst her body was definitely saying something else. In the end her decision to get out of the car was prompted by fear alone. Accepting someone else into her life meant another person to worry about. Another person to potentially lose. Not only was Alasdair someone who'd given up on her before, but he also put himself in harm's way every day of the week, increasing the odds of leaving her behind just as her parents and Iain had.

She'd come back here to rediscover herself, not run headlong into making another mistake.

'I know this wasn't planned but I didn't hear either of us complaining.' Everything Alasdair was saying with that twinkle in his eye was true, but she didn't want to complicate her life again. She'd learned a long, hard lesson about rushing into relationships. The whole idea of coming home was to be true to who she was, not get swept away by the idea of romance again. Especially when their history was already so troubled. Loving and losing again was not something she was ready to do any time soon.

'Anyway, I'm not going to push you into anything. I had a good time with you today and we're contractually obliged to keep doing it until Christmas.'

That made her laugh and she was thankful he was able to keep things light and not demand any sort of commitment from her when she wasn't able to give him any. Even if she really, really enjoyed kissing him.

'I'll see you next time, Santa.' She waved him goodbye, bracing herself for the onslaught of questions and taunts from Chrissie once she walked inside.

'Later, Elfie.' He was still smiling, so at least she hadn't insulted him by turning down his proposition. For now. Only time would tell how long she'd manage to resist.

Alasdair had to adjust himself for the drive home, uncomfortable after that red-hot encounter with Shona had come to an abrupt end. He guessed there was still some of that teenage boy left in him after all to have carried on like that with her in public without a care for anything other than how she was making him feel. Horny. Despite what he'd said, he knew the ferocity of the passion had taken them both by surprise. Yes, he'd been flirting and teasing her, and that chemistry was stronger than ever, but their kiss had been on a different level.

He turned on the air con to try and cool down as he drove home. Today had been a rollercoaster ride for him between his dad and Shona. Being with her balanced out all the negative energy generated by his father but it didn't make his emotions any less muddled.

He meant what he said about not pushing her into anything because he was at a loss to make sense of what he wanted too. Having another relationship was a step he'd sworn he'd never make and, as much as his libido wanted Shona at any cost, he had to remain cautious. Getting carried away only led to heartache and it had taken him years to recover from the last devastation.

They had history, but she'd spent most of her adult life with her husband. He'd been leading a happy life on Braelin until now. For him to put everything on the line for another relationship he'd have to be sure it was what they both wanted. Not simply a poor substitute for someone else. If that was the case, he'd rather remain single.

It was important for him to remember that not everyone got their happy-ever-after. No matter how much he might want it, there was always a chance he'd end up bitter, twisted and alone like his father.

'Don't say a word,' Shona warned, walking straight past Chrissie into the house.

'Oh, no, you don't. I want details!'

'You saw what happened. We kissed. I left. That's it.' That was where she wanted to leave it, but Chrissie was tracking her through the house like a bloodhound refusing to back away from its potential reward at the end of a hunt.

'That was not just a kiss or else I've been seriously missing out. You were literally steaming up the windows.'

Shona went into the bedroom and slammed the door shut on the conversation. Mainly because she was still recovering from said kiss. She flopped down on the edge of her bed, her jelly-filled legs unable to carry her any longer.

Chrissie apparently didn't see a closed door as a deterrent and opened it to continue her commentary.

'You know, I'm not sure Mrs Claus would be happy for you to be snogging the big man.'

'Well, you can tell her it's a one-off. No need to call the divorce lawyers just yet.'

'And is it a one-off? That looked pretty hot and heavy for a first kiss.'

'Technically, that wasn't our first kiss, but it has to be our last.'

'Why?'

'Chrissie, you're getting as bad as the twins with your questions. I'm not getting involved with anyone. Now, can I get changed, please? In private.'

There was no chance of that happening as the girls ran in and jumped on the bed, almost bouncing Shona off it.

'Auntie Shona, why are you wearing that?'

'Auntie Shona, do you know Santa?'

'I…er…' With pleading eyes, she sought her sister's help on this one. She didn't want to say anything that could potentially jeopardise the girls' enjoyment of Christmas. Believing in the magic was what childhood was all about and she'd have loved to be getting her own little ones excited about the holidays.

She thought of Alasdair and how the chance for him to have a child had been taken away from him too. They'd both had their troubles and all the more reason why starting something would be a huge mistake. There was too much baggage involved.

'Girls, you have to promise you can keep a secret.' Chrissie commanded nods from her daughters before she continued. 'Auntie Shona is working as one of Santa's elves this year. She has a very important job.'

This information drew gasps and oohs from the excited little girls.

'Does that mean you know Santa, Auntie Shona?'

'Can we meet him, Auntie Shona?'

'Of course you can. Auntie Shona can bring him home any time she likes.' Chrissie was smiling smugly as she dropped her right in it.

'Why would you do that to me?' Shona asked

when the twins ran off gabbling about Christmas lists and reindeer.

Chrissie rested her hands on Shona's shoulders and gave her a shake. 'Because you, dear sister, don't know what's good for you. Alasdair is one of the best and he clearly fancies you rotten. I'm just giving you a little nudge in the right direction.'

Shona couldn't bring herself to argue any more when she knew Chrissie was just looking out for her.

'I only want you to be happy, to have a life of your own, and I know you like him. If you really don't want him to come here, I'll find a way to let the girls down gently.' She must have mistaken Shona's silence as seething rage as she rapidly backpedalled.

'It's okay,' Shona said wearily. Constantly battling her feelings for Alasdair was tiring. Especially after today, when she'd learned so much more about him and herself, after one kiss spiralled into something so much more dangerous and exciting. 'I wouldn't want to disappoint the girls. Or you.'

They hugged it out but agreeing to this absolutely did not mean she and Alasdair were in any way an item. She'd make that perfectly clear before she asked him for the favour and hoped he didn't expect anything in return.

* * *

'Alasdair? It's Shona.'

'Hey. Long time, no see. It's been what, forty minutes?' He hadn't been expecting her to be in touch so soon. A small, optimistic part of him was hoping it was because she wanted to pick up where they'd left off in the car, but he had to be realistic. They were both too scarred by the past to blindly rush into anything.

'Yeah, sorry. I know you probably just want to have a lie down after today but I need to ask you a favour.' Her apologetic tone and slight hesitation suggested she wasn't entirely comfortable asking him for anything.

'Sure. What is it you need?'

'Well, it's Chrissie's fault, really… She promised the girls Santa would come over and see them. I wondered if you might call in some time to say hello to them? Sorry, I know you're busy—'

'It's no problem. When do you want me to come over?'

'Oh, there's no hurry. They've got it into their heads I'm working with Santa…they saw the costume, you see. Anyway, it'll make their night if I can tell them they're going to get a private meeting with the man himself.' Her sweet laugh almost made him wish she was asking him over because she wanted to see him, be with him.

Regardless of everything he'd been telling himself that getting involved would be a bad idea.

'I could come over now, if you like? I've still got the suit on.' It might seem over-keen, but he'd rather be seeing Shona again than spending another night sitting here on his own. Especially when he had such hot memories of her today to torture him in the dark.

'I can't ask you to do that. You've been out all day. It wouldn't be fair to make you drive back out here.'

'It's no problem. You're not exactly miles away. I was going to call at the boathouse anyway.' He wasn't but she shouldn't feel guilty about something he wanted to do.

'Only if you're sure…'

'I won't stay too long. I'll just read them a bedtime story or something.'

'That would be lovely. Thanks, Alasdair.'

When he hung up the phone it was all he could do not to jump in the car and race over at once, but he had a little dignity left. It would be nice to spend more time with Shona. And make the girls' night special, of course. He simply had to make sure he didn't outstay his welcome.

CHAPTER SEVEN

'SIT DOWN. YOU CAN'T possibly tidy anything more.' Chrissie directed her towards the sofa, but Shona was as giddy as the girls at the prospect of a visit from Santa.

'I didn't think he was going to come over right now.' She'd hardly had time to recover from their earlier encounter, dashing around to gather all the toys lying around before he arrived. Not that she'd be able to sit still anyway. It was as though an entire swarm of bees had set up home inside her, the buzzing in her ears almost deafening and her body positively vibrating with anticipation. Although, strictly speaking, he wasn't coming to see her.

'What does that tell you? He clearly can't get enough of you.' Hearing her sister say it started a renewed wave of nerves inside Shona about what was happening between her and Alasdair. She'd told him she didn't want to start anything but deep down she was worried it was already too late.

'Or he's just very good at his job.' Shona refuted Chrissie's version of events because to believe it would scare the life out of her.

'Look, Auntie Shona.' Tilly and Marie rushed into the living room to show her the pictures they'd been fastidiously painting since she had told them Santa was coming to visit. They were both in their red-and-cream pyjamas covered in reindeer, having been bathed without a hint of dissention tonight. At this rate Chrissie would be making her call Alasdair every night to come over.

She studied the brightly coloured splodges sliding down the paper and beamed at her nieces. 'I'm sure Santa is going to love them. Why don't you leave them on the kitchen table to dry then go and brush your teeth for bed?'

The suddenly obedient twosome toddled off to do as they were told, leaving their mother staring after them in disbelief. 'Why can't it be Christmas all year round?'

'Because it would cost a fortune and mean I'd have to wear this ridiculous outfit permanently.' Not to mention the hours she'd have to put in alongside Alasdair. There was no way she'd survive all that time together and come out unscathed.

The rap at the front door almost sent her into cardiac arrest.

'That's him.' She stood staring at Chrissie as though she'd been caught doing something she shouldn't have.

'Go and open the door, then, or are you waiting for him to come down the chimney?'

'Right. Yes.' In her panic she'd forgotten it was she who'd actually asked him to come over. She checked her rosy cheeks in the hallway mirror and straightened her elf ears before she opened the door.

Alasdair would be unrecognisable to the children in his fat suit and beard, but she would have known those eyes anywhere.

'Ho, ho, ho!' he boomed loud enough for the little ones to hear and come screaming down the stairs.

'Hello, Santa. Thanks for taking the time out of your very busy schedule to visit two special little girls who I hope are sitting quietly and behaving themselves right now.' Shona raised her voice so the twins could hear her. More squeals and the thundering sound of running feet could be heard as they took up their places in the living room.

'I really appreciate this,' she whispered as he walked in.

'No problem. It's nice to find people who're

happy to see me.' His comment played a sad lament on her heart strings, thinking that was why he was enjoying his new role so much.

The twins were wide-eyed as he walked into the living room, as was their mother. 'I do hope Shona is managing to stay on the nice list this year, Santa,' Chrissie said. 'I heard she was a bit naughty today.'

Shona was tight-lipped and tempted to kick her sister with one of her pointy shoes at the reference to their earlier tryst. She could do without being reminded of it, especially when Alasdair was in the room.

'Not at all. She was very, very nice.'

Shona was glad she'd already painted her cheeks so her furious blushing would hopefully go unnoticed. Thankfully, the girls were so entranced by the sight of Father Christmas in their living room they were paying no attention to anything the adults were saying.

Santa Alasdair walked over to where the twins were sitting by the Christmas tree and kneeled down to talk to them. 'I heard there were two good girls who deserved an early Christmas present.'

Two eager little blonde heads nodded in agreement with everything he said.

'There's one for you and one for you.' He reached into his sack and pulled out two of the little gift boxes he'd taken to the nursing home earlier.

'Thank you, Santa,' they chorused before pulling the ribbons off to reveal the contents— little toddler-sized cookies.

'You can have one now but then you'll have to brush your teeth again,' Chrissie conceded as they stared at the cookies with unbridled longing.

'I heard there were two more good girls in the house.' When he presented Shona and Chrissie with boxes of their own, Shona swore her heart grew two sizes bigger.

'That's so thoughtful of you, Santa. Isn't it, Shona?'

'Very.' She was clutching the homemade gift to her chest and willing herself not to tear up at the gesture. He'd become such a caring man over the years it was a pity no one had apparently repaid him in kind. She wondered how many presents he'd received as a child and how many were under his Christmas tree now? There and then she resolved to do something special for him to mark the occasion and let him know his thoughtfulness was appreciated.

'Shona said you might read the girls a bedtime story?' Chrissie did her best to move proceedings along so they could get the children to bed as soon as possible.

'Yes, so if they go and get ready for bed, I'll read this to them.' He reached into his bag again and pulled out a gorgeous hardback book of Christmas stories.

Chrissie shooed the twins off to get ready for bed, leaving Shona alone with Alasdair.

'That's a beautiful edition. I hope you didn't buy it specially for tonight.' It looked expensive, and from everything she'd witnessed today she wouldn't have put it past him to have gone the extra mile for story time either.

He stroked the cover, decorated with embossed golden stars, and looked a little wistful as he did so. 'No, I had this one at home. It's silly really. After my ex told me she was pregnant this was the first thing I went out and bought. I had this picture of us all sitting around on Christmas Eve reading it before we put out milk and cookies for Santa. It was my idea of the perfect family Christmas I never had as a child.'

Shona had to restrain herself from reaching out to hug him. It wasn't a big ask from someone who gave so much, but he'd been denied it in such a cruel fashion. She'd been lucky to have the kind of Christmases with her family that he'd only ever dreamed about. It wasn't even that they had loads of money to splurge on toys or food, but the happy memories were just of everyone being together, loving each other. Something which had obviously been lacking throughout Alasdair's life. It meant even more that he was willing to come and make someone else's children's dreams come true.

When he went to the twins' room Shona followed and hovered by the door as he settled into a chair by their beds. The girls were riveted by his storytelling. As was she. He had voices for each character, knew how to draw out the drama and had all in the room hanging on his every word. They were sad when he finished the story and closed the book.

'More,' the twins begged, clutching their dolls under the covers.

'Sorry, girls. I have to go and feed the reindeer, but I'll be back on Christmas Eve, if you're very good for your mother and your aunt,' he said with a wink in her direction.

The girls insisted on giving him a hug before he left and she could tell Alasdair was touched by the gesture, his voice a little choked up as he said his goodbyes. Shona left Chrissie to get the twins settled again and saw Alasdair out to the door.

'Would you like to stay for a drink or anything? It seems wrong to send you home again after coming over and doing that for us.'

'It's fine. I enjoyed it. It might confuse the

wee ones if I hang around. I wouldn't want to spoil the magic for them.'

In that moment Shona knew beyond doubt he would have made a wonderful father. He cared so much and knew what not to do in order to make children happy. At least when she'd married Iain she'd known what she'd agreed to. Her childless state was of her own doing, but Alasdair had been hurt in the worst way. To have been told he was going to be a father then have it all ripped away from him without any thought for his feelings must have been devastating for him.

'Well, thanks for coming. I'm sure they won't stop talking about that until Christmas. Thanks for the presents too. That was a very special touch.' She'd make sure to get him something in return to express her thanks.

'No problem. Maybe we can get that drink some other time?' He took off his hat and beard, so she knew it was Alasdair talking and Santa wasn't angling for a date. Her defences had crumbled a little more tonight with every glimpse of his vulnerability when reminded of his background. He wouldn't want to get hurt again any more than she did, and having a drink together seemed harmless enough.

'That would be nice.' After everything he'd done here tonight, it was the least she could do.

Tonight she'd really seen the softer side of Alasdair Murray and completely erased that idea of him purposely wanting to cause anybody pain.

He broke into a beautiful smile. 'Good. I'll hold you to that and we'll fit it in somewhere between our next community service duties.'

They stood on the doorstep in silence then for a fraction too long to be comfortable, so she made the move to end the night. 'I guess I'll see you at the next official Christmas engagement, then.'

'Goodnight, Shona.' He leaned forward to kiss her on the cheek and Shona eagerly met him for that one last connection. Something she could hold on to when she went to sleep.

The kiss was brief but neither moved back to claim their own personal space. That contact spurred something to life. A reminder of kisses in their childhood and the not so distant past. She could feel the change between them. Electricity buzzing in the air as though they'd flicked a switch and brought something back to life.

His breath was hot on her skin; his cheek pressed against hers. Alasdair dropped everything he was carrying to wind his arms around her waist. He didn't need to pull her as hard as he did, for she would have gone willingly. Still, it was proof his desire was as great as hers for this to happen again.

Lips on lips now, they'd stopped pretending this was merely a goodbye, to indulge in the kiss they'd apparently both been waiting for. Slow, long and sensuous, it was different to the one they'd shared earlier. Deeper, more meaningful perhaps because of the time they'd spent together tonight with her family. It was the first time he'd really become part of her world. Before now he'd simply skirted on the periphery—at school, on the beach, anywhere but in her home. This time the kiss and the mixed-up feelings behind it were real.

When it ended and they pulled apart Alasdair looked as sheepish as she felt at having given into temptation so quickly after the last time. He opened his mouth to say something, then closed it again, picked up his stuff and gave her a wave as he walked away.

Shona floated to bed clutching her present and the memory of that soft kiss fresh on her lips. She was sure she was as happy as the two little girls in the next room after Alasdair's visit as she snuggled down under the covers.

Then somewhere in the distance she swore she heard a siren, and that contentment which had settled inside her began to lurch violently. It was a sobering reminder that the family-minded, Santa-playing Alasdair also rushed out into the darkness to venture across the sea, no matter the dangers. He wasn't the safe option her heart should get too attached to.

With work, and two over-excited nieces to contend with, Shona had a couple of days to get over that day and night she'd spent in Alasdair's company. The kissing and the rush of blood in her veins every time he touched her began to lose some of its potency when she imagined herself sitting wide awake in bed wondering if he'd come home safely from that call-out. She'd seen him from a distance the next day, so she could stop worrying about him on that occasion, but she knew it would become an ongoing concern if she didn't back away now. The last thing she needed was to fall for someone and lose them again. She'd been through that too many times to sacrifice the peace of her single life now.

Today, however, was going to be a major test.

'Are you ready to go?' Alasdair came to meet her on the jetty, climbing out of the boat she was supposed to join him on. He'd borrowed it from one of his crewmates to transport them to the mainland, so they weren't tied to the infrequent timetable of the ferry. To say she was anxious about the journey on such a small vessel would have been an understatement. This was the first time she'd set foot on a fishing boat since her father's accident, convinced the same fate might befall her and whoever else was on board. It showed her trust in Alasdair's abilities that she'd agreed to this at all. Especially with only the two of them travelling. They weren't ideal conditions for maintaining a distance from the man who was never far from her thoughts.

'I wouldn't say ready. Resigned, perhaps. I'm a little unclear about what we're supposed to be doing when we get there.' The vague instructions, once they'd agreed on a day they could both take off, had merely been to bring her elf costume to change into later.

'We're the promotions team. We're whipping up interest so Braelin gets the visitors to the Winter Wonderland. There's always an ad in the paper, and the requisite social media blitz, but there's nothing like having Santa and his elf handing out leaflets in the centre of Glasgow.'

'I'm sure we'll make quite the spectacle,' she said as he took her hand and helped her inside the boat.

'There's a lifejacket for you to put on in case of an emergency.'

She snapped her head up at that one. The sea wasn't somewhere she was ever happy to be and this was setting off alarm bells as well as unsettling her stomach. 'Why would I need a lifejacket? You do know how to steer this thing, don't you?'

'It's just a precaution, that's all. I've had plenty of practice sailing boats, don't worry.' He reached under the seat and handed her a fetching bright orange life preserver. 'I can help you put it on if you need a hand.'

'I think I can manage, thank you.' Even the thought of him tying the straps around her waist, his breath hot on her neck, was enough to make her wish she wasn't going to have to wear an extra layer. She was already enveloped in a thick wool jumper to keep out the cold she'd imagined she'd be experiencing out at sea in December. Winter in Scotland meant always being prepared for extreme weather. As well as her elf outfit, her holdall contained a hat, scarf, gloves and a spare pair of thick socks. If only she'd thought to pack a bargepole to keep Alasdair away from her personal space at all times. Impossible in the cramped confines of this compact vessel.

'Okay, hold on while I get us out of here.' He commanded the wheel with such confidence and authority he could have been the captain of a cruise liner. The old denims he was wearing along with his cream fisherman's chunky knit sweater were as sexy as any uniform.

She took a seat and hung on for her life as

the boat tore out of the harbour. They were skimming through the waves, the spray whipping across her face and refreshing her after the long shift she'd worked the day before. If she stopped stressing about her roller-coaster emotions around Alasdair, and they didn't die at sea, this could turn out to be a pleasant trip.

'It's been a while since I've had a proper day off. Usually, I'm helping Chrissie with the girls when I'm not working. Not that I'm complaining. I spent long enough on my own before I moved back. I'm lucky Chrissie agreed to take me in, and I love being part of the chaos.'

'I enjoyed being part of your family chaos the other night.' He'd steered the conversation back to his visit and events which she'd been trying to avoid for the sake of her mental health. It was on the tip of her tongue to give him an open-ended invitation to stop by any time for dinner, but common sense won out over her heart.

'The girls were thrilled. Christmas is all about the children, but being in a house with little ones again gives me an excuse to get excited about it too. The tree-decorating, the presents and the whole build-up to Christmas Eve is really heightened for me this year. Made even more special now I'm one of Santa's helpers. I think that's really scored me a lot of extra cool points with my nieces.'

'I'm glad you're reconnecting with your family. It's important. Especially at this time of year. I don't think I ever lost my enthusiasm for the season. Despite the lack of festive cheer in my upbringing, and the lack of family to do it for, I love it. It might seem a bit sad to go to all the trouble of decorating just for myself, but it makes the place more homely.'

'No, I get that. I used to love putting all the fairy lights and stockings up. Iain always thought it was a bit overboard and pointless for two fully grown adults.'

She and Chrissie had left cookies and milk for Santa right up until she moved away. Their mother had continued to leave surprise gifts for them under the tree and kept the magic alive all that time. It was marrying Iain which had forced her to grow up. Only then had she realised how special her mother had been with their Christmas traditions. Something she thought no one else would ever understand. Especially when she had no children of her own to carry on those traditions legitimately.

'If I had my way you'd wear that outfit all the time.'

'You know that's weird, right?' They were back to teasing each other and it served to show the differences between Alasdair and Iain. Where she doubted Iain had ever enjoyed the over-commercialisation of the season, it was clear Alasdair was keen to experience it properly for the first time. With family.

'Everyone has their kink,' he said, turning around from the wheel to wink at her.

Shona knew he was joking but the tongue-in-cheek comment was suggestive enough for her to consider donning it now just for him. Thankfully, the good old Scottish weather stepped in to save her from herself. The rain started from nowhere, lashing down upon them without mercy.

'I thought the forecast said it would be dry today.' She had to shout to be heard over the heavy shower beating the hull of the boat like a drum.

'Mainly dry, with a chance of rain,' Alasdair corrected. 'They made sure to cover their bases. Why don't you go down below and keep dry? I can handle things up here.'

She did as he said but only to retrieve some of the wet gear for him to put on in an attempt to protect him from the elements. Once she'd donned her waterproofs she went back on deck and handed him his. 'Here, put this on or you'll catch your death.'

She helped him into the gear whilst he tried to keep control of the wheel. The boat was tilting and lurching now as the wind whipped up the waves around them. 'Stay below, Shona. It's gonna get rough for a while up here.'

She didn't want to leave him to deal with everything on his own but neither did she need him worrying about her when he was trying to keep them upright. It wasn't easy keeping her balance as she made her way down the steps, being thrown from side to side, but at least she was dry down here. The swell of nausea rising in her was more for their safety than the rocking motion of the boat. Her anticipation and anxiety over spending a day in close proximity to Alasdair had overtaken her fear of the sea, but with each passing minute that was changing. It was only a small vessel, powerless against Mother Nature if she chose to display her might, and Shona wouldn't last five minutes in the sea. She was relying completely on Alasdair to navigate them both to safety.

There was no way she could sit here as though she were on a pleasure cruise, waiting until they made dry land before sticking her head above the parapet. Her conscience would never allow it. As she wove her way back up the few steps she thought she could hear him shouting.

'Is there something wrong?' she called to him against the wind.

'I've had a message from the coastguard. There's a medical emergency on one of the outlying islands. We're the closest to it until they can launch the lifeboat or get the helicopter out here. Do you mind if we make a slight detour?'

'Not at all. Can we get there safely?' Hearing that they could end this perilous journey soon was already having a calming effect on her stomach, if not the weather.

'Well, it's closer than the mainland and the bay should be more sheltered compared to how exposed it is out here. We could wait out the storm there once we make an assessment on the casualty.'

'Do we have any information on what we're walking, or sailing, into?'

'Duncan Laird is the sole inhabitant out there, apart from his sheep. He's had a fall and he's lying there somewhere, unable to move and exposed to the elements.'

'He has his own island? Wow.' She had visions of a character who'd been shipwrecked there decades ago, his hair and beard bedraggled and sun-bleached, wearing clothes he'd fashioned himself from leaves and assorted fauna.

Alasdair chuckled. 'It's not quite the tropical paradise you might be picturing. Basically, it's a scrap of land his family have owned for generations, mostly used for grazing livestock, but he's a bit of a hermit. Prefers animals to the company of humans. His nephew comes out to check on him occasionally.'

'Sounds like quite a character.'

'Oh, he is. I've met him a couple of times when we've had to pick up a few shipwrecked or stranded fishermen who've got in trouble out that way. He never appreciates unexpected visitors.'

'In that case he's gonna love us.' In Shona's experience older men weren't always keen to accept they had a problem at the best of times. They didn't know what condition Mr Laird was currently in, but they might have trouble getting him to co-operate if he was conscious.

'I'm sure you can sweet talk him around, and if all else fails we can always play dress-up again.' Alasdair navigated the boat into a nook partially sheltered from the storm on the shingle beach. He grabbed the first-aid kit on board before helping Shona back onto dry land. Despite the isolated, stark surroundings of winter-stripped trees against grey skies, she was grateful to have made it ashore here safely. All thanks to Alasdair.

Without thinking she threw her arms around his neck and squeezed him tight. 'Thank you so much for keeping me safe.'

'Er—it's okay. I don't think we were in any real danger.'

She ignored his protest to prolong the warm feel of him pressed against her. The smell of the salty sea mixed with his musky aftershave filled her senses and she let out a little sigh of contentment. It was one thing telling herself she shouldn't get involved when he was miles away out at sea. Quite another when she was in his arms, trusting him with her life.

CHAPTER EIGHT

'THE COTTAGE IS just over the hill if you're okay to do a spot of climbing?' He slowly peeled her off from around his person and held out a hand to her as he began the ascent up the grassy, muddy incline.

'I'm beginning to think I should have stayed at home, or at least put in a shift in a warm, dry hospital department,' she grumbled as he forced her back to the real world. Where she had to worry about what might happen to Alasdair out there in the wilds and not simply how good it felt to be holding him.

'And miss all the excitement?' He tutted. 'The old Shona would've walked the length and breadth of Braelin with me over that summer and wouldn't care about a bit of rain.'

The reminder of their enduring chemistry started her insides rolling again as if she were still on that storm-tossed boat. Rediscovering the 'old Shona' had been behind her reasons for coming here. Part of that might just be accepting she still had feelings for Alasdair. That teenage girl who would have followed him anywhere was obviously still there. There was no one else who could have convinced her to dress as an elf, sail to the mainland in nothing more than a dinghy, or go mountaineering as part of the rescue services.

She slid on the wet ground, coating her boot in a thick layer of brown mud. 'The key word there being "summer". Our exploits might've been quite different if we'd been spending time together at this time of year.'

'I don't know…we managed to generate our own heat without a problem. I think we would've managed to be together whatever the weather.'

Once again he managed to make her think about the carefree people they'd been. They'd have danced in the rain, rolled around in the snow or found shelter from the wind as long as they'd been together. Even now, without the patient waiting for their medical intervention, she'd rather have been by his side up to her ankles in a swamp than sitting alone on the shore.

'Well, luckily for Mr Laird, our time apart helped us to learn important medical skills. I doubt we would've been much help to anyone if we'd stayed joined at the hip.' Back then her thoughts had been completely consumed by

Alasdair. If they'd developed a relationship beyond that summer, it was possible she'd have ended up a pregnant teenager before a too-young marriage to him instead of Iain. She tried not to dwell on whether or not she would have preferred that homely life to her career and living in the city. There was nothing that could turn back time and change what had happened.

The tumbledown cottage which came into view prevented any further nostalgic wallowing. 'Somebody actually lives in that?'

The stone building may have been white-washed at some point but now had an unattractive green sludge bleeding into the brickwork. A rotted wooden door with only the ghost of red paint visible on it barely hung on its hinges. The path up to it was nothing more than another trail of sludge. The only welcoming feature was the curl of smoke trailing from the chimney.

'As Duncan will tell you, it's functional and he owns it. That's all that matters to him. His nephew, Liam, makes sure he has everything he needs in terms of food and fuel.' Alasdair gave a cursory knock on the front door before letting them in.

'Hello? Duncan? It's Alasdair Murray. I've got Shona here with me too. She's a nurse,' he called ahead in the gloom. Shona wondered for a moment if there was even any electricity out here when the hallway was so dark. It was like something out of a horror movie, walking into the silent unknown, and she followed closely behind Alasdair as he announced their arrival.

'I take it he hasn't been able to make his way back. We don't know exactly where he fell. I don't think his phone signal was that great.'

'He couldn't be too far away if the fire's still going. We should take a look out the back,' Shona suggested. The dark sky wouldn't make him easy to spot. Especially with no obvious source of outdoor lighting. They needed to find him and treat him as soon as possible.

Alasdair led the way through the small kitchen and out the back door. Any hope Shona had that they'd find him nearby vanished when she saw the vast acreage of land leading away from the cottage. She'd expected a little cottage garden, maybe a few chickens scratching at the ground, but there seemed to be no visible boundaries as far as the eye could see. It was going to be difficult to locate Mr Laird in the fading light.

'Duncan? Can you hear us out there?' Alasdair's unexpected yell literally made Shona jump into action. She set off in the opposition direction to him, calling and scanning the area for signs of life in the descending gloom.

'Mr Laird? If you can hear us raise your hand

or call out.' She had no idea if he was capable of doing either, but any movement or sound might help pinpoint their patient.

Alasdair wandered off towards some nearby grazing sheep, while Shona decided to make her way around what was left of a hedge around the perimeter of the area. In some places it was overgrown and sprawling and there were gaps where it had been trodden down, but she figured it would help her keep track of the area she was covering. It might help her to find her way back in the dark if it came to it too.

'Mr Laird? Help is here but we need you to tell us where you are.' She kept one hand outstretched to map her progress along the straggly border as she made her way further and further away from the light of the cottage.

For a moment she thought she heard a soft moan and stopped to listen. In the distance she could hear the sheep bleating their disapproval at Alasdair disturbing their supper, but there was a sound closer. A moan she could barely hear above the pounding of her heart. She moved towards the source, having to clamber over rocks and the remains of a broken-down fence. That was when she saw the dark shape lying on the ground.

'Alasdair! Over here!' she shouted, waving frantically to grab his attention. Once she was sure he was on his way over, she kneeled down beside the figure sprawled awkwardly before her.

'Mr Laird? Can you hear me?'

He groaned but at least he was conscious.

The first thing she saw when she examined him were his torn trousers and the gash on his leg. He'd obviously been bleeding for some time, his clothes and the ground beneath stained crimson from his injury.

'My name is Shona. I'm a nurse at Braelin Hospital and I'm here to help you. You've had a fall.' The ground was uneven here and she could see scraps of material caught in some barbed wire not far from where he was lying. It didn't take a genius to work out what had happened.

Alasdair arrived beside her, having sprinted over to assist. The first thing he did was strip off his coat and cover Mr Laird to keep him warm. 'How is he?'

'Conscious but with a nasty leg wound. I don't know if he hit his head when he fell but the ground seems soft enough to have prevented any serious damage.'

'We probably shouldn't move him anyway until help arrives. If you're okay to examine him here, I'll go and see what I can find to clean that wound.'

'I'm not sure I could move you, Mr Laird, even if I had to,' Shona said to the patient as she was left alone with him. It was important to continue talking to him and keep him conscious and responsive for the best outcome.

She bundled her own coat under his feet, careful not to move his legs about too much but needing to elevate them above his heart to keep the blood circulating to his vital organs. They had no idea how long he'd been lying out here and there was a danger of shock setting into the body. Especially when he'd lost so much blood. She pulled his eyelids up and found his pupils dilated. Listened to his chest, where his breathing was rapid and shallow. His weak, racing pulse was another sign that that was exactly what was happening. A body going into shock meant there mightn't be enough blood getting to the organs and tissues, leading to possible organ failure along with life-threatening consequences.

'We're going to have to get you to hospital for treatment.' There they could run all the tests necessary to find out exactly what the problem was in case he had other underlying health problems which had caused him to fall, such as a problem with his blood pressure. Although he looked a fit and healthy man, goodness knew when he'd last had a health check-up.

'No hospitals,' he grumbled. He was conscious enough to complain, which was a good sign.

'Are you on any medication, Mr Laird?'

'No.' It was information she could pass on to the medical team who'd be treating him once he left the island so they knew any drugs he received wouldn't be interfering with any other treatment.

'How are you both holding up?' Alasdair returned then with his arms full of supplies, and she was glad to see her companion returning so they could work together to keep Mr Laird talking or complaining. Whatever it took in order to help him survive this ordeal.

'I think he's going into shock but he's responsive, if a little tetchy.'

'Don't worry, the coastguard isn't far away. I've given them directions, so they're going to land as close as possible. I've got hot water and some cloths to clean that wound and bandages to dress it. He's going to need stitches and probably a tetanus injection.' He rolled his sleeves up and began to clean away the dirt and blood around the injury site. At least the blood wasn't spurting out, so Alasdair's assessment that all he'd need was stitches seemed accurate. It was reassuring having someone else with medical knowledge around in such circumstances.

He was a calming, supportive presence Shona hadn't had in her life for a long time. Alasdair respected her expertise, offering assistance instead of trying to take over.

'No doctors,' their reluctant patient muttered and began squirming under their attentions.

'Duncan? It's Alasdair Murray here. You've had a nasty fall and we're just patching you up until help gets here.'

'No hospital,' the gaunt figure on the ground reiterated, though his words weren't as clear as they could have been.

'Now, Duncan, this isn't just something you can fix on your own. You need to go to hospital for treatment. They'll get you back on your feet in no time.'

Mr Laird grumbled again but no longer put up any sort of fight as Alasdair dressed the wound as best he could.

They heard the whirr of the chopper blades and were blinded by the searchlights as help arrived close by.

Shona watched as they landed in the clearing behind the cottage and members of the crew exited, pushing a stretcher towards them.

'Does this happen as often as it seems?' she asked Alasdair. He was clearly used to this level of drama in his life, but she could do without the life-or-death scenarios outside of the hospital. She had her fair share of emergencies at work, but he seemed to be permanently on duty. There was no rest for him or her nerves when the nature of his noble job meant they were constantly on edge.

'We don't usually have medevac situations so close together but the weather in winter can be so unpredictable, as you know. I'm afraid we don't get to pick and choose what happens out here.' Alasdair helped with the neck brace and back board as the paramedics got ready to transport Duncan whilst Shona relayed all the information she had so far. Once they loaded the stretcher into the back of the helicopter she was able to relax a little, knowing she'd done her job and now it was someone else's turn to look after the patient.

There were one or two hairy moments as the helicopter was buffeted by the wind, and Shona huffed out a breath of relief when they finally flew away with their patient safely on board.

Without the guiding lights from the chopper they were left out in the field in the now pitch-black darkness. Alasdair used the light from his phone to illuminate their path back to the cottage.

'Hold on to my arm. I don't want you stumbling about and falling in the dark too.' He didn't need to tell her twice. Goodness knew how long it would be before the helicopter would be available to pick up another casualty in the wilderness.

Although she couldn't see it now, she could hear and feel the squelch of mud beneath her boots. She clung tighter to Alasdair, wrapping her hands around his impressive bicep and jamming her body up against his as the renewed force of the gale tried its best to knock her off her feet. Then the heavens opened, and the rain didn't take any time before pouring down on them. It came on so fast, so heavy, they were soaked through in seconds.

'What are we going to do?' Shona had redeployed her coat as a make-do shelter over their heads, but the run-off had drenched her back and gone down her legs.

'Get someplace dry hopefully.' Alasdair sounded as happy as she was about their current predicament.

'No, I mean about the trip. It's probably too late to catch Glasgow shoppers now. Given the choice, no one in their right minds would be out in this weather.'

'We're not going anywhere. Sailing out there, on that boat, in that weather, would be a disaster waiting to happen.' He unlatched the cottage door and stood back to let her inside. Although it seemed a pointless exercise now, when they were leaving puddles with every step, she shook the pool of water out of her coat before entering. She squeezed a river out of the ends of her hair and tried to wipe off the layer of water on her face, but every part of her was sopping wet.

'What are you saying? How are we going to get home?' The consequences of what he'd told her were just beginning to sink in. If the conditions were too bad for them to go to the mainland, they were also so dangerous they couldn't possibly go back either.

'We're not going anywhere until the weather improves and it's safe for us to do so. I'm afraid we're going to have to rest up here for a while.'

'No!' The ferocity of her denial surprised even her, but the idea that they should be stuck here for the night was completely unacceptable to Shona.

'We don't have any choice.' Alasdair looked a little wounded by her reaction. Shona simply couldn't stay here, alone, with Alasdair. That definitely hadn't been in her plans.

'B-but how? Where? How?' She glanced around the meagre surroundings with the one tiny bedroom leading off from the living room and thought she'd rather take her chances out at sea than be expected to spend the night with him here. It would be less dangerous. Because she didn't appear to have much control over her actions or emotions these days.

'We'll figure that out after we get dried off. If you could have a look for some towels and blankets, I'll try and get the fire going again. I don't think Duncan has central heating out here.' He was trying to make light of their situation whilst being proactive, but she was more concerned about resisting temptation than staying warm. At least they'd be starting off in different directions. She left him scrabbling about in the hearth with kindling and matches to investigate Mr Laird's bedroom.

It felt intrusive going through someone else's belongings and she wasn't comfortable doing it. The bedroom furniture was solid wood, probably handed down through generations of the Laird family. She pulled out the heavy and cumbersome drawers, which were ultimately devoid of anything useful for their impromptu stay. On the floor behind the bedroom door she found a rustic oak chest which, when she opened it, she found contained a pile of thick woollen blankets. There were even bags of dried lavender inside to ensure they didn't smell fusty. She eagerly gathered up her spoils to show Alasdair. If nothing else, this payload meant they wouldn't have to lie together to generate body heat the way they did in the movies.

'It's warmer in here now.' The sight of the flickering flames in the hearth when Shona walked back into the living room was very welcome.

Alasdair pounded his chest and attempted a caveman impression as he pointed towards his achievement. 'Me make fire.'

'Well, me found blankets,' she said, acknowledging her part in saving them from potential hypothermia.

'There's a couple of towels there too. I found some in the bathroom.' He pointed to a few threadbare, discoloured towels which at least looked clean. Shona would take them. She felt as though she would never dry out.

'Great. I hope he won't mind us helping ourselves to his stuff while he's absent.' She grabbed up one of the towels and began to dry her hair with it.

'I'll explain things to him and bring him some supplies out. That should smooth out any ruffled feathers. Although I think in the circumstances he'd forgive us for making ourselves at home. We're only here because he needed help.'

It was true but she couldn't help wondering what would have happened if they'd sailed on and got stuck out there in the storm. The thought of bobbing about in the vast seas made her shudder with horror.

'We need to get out of these wet clothes and warm up before we catch our deaths.' Alasdair understandably assumed she was shivering because of the cold.

'I might go and change in the bathroom.' The idea of stripping down here seemed a little too intimate. She helped herself to another towel and one of the blankets, knowing it was all she was going to have to preserve her modesty unless she raided Duncan's wardrobe too.

'You could, but it's so cold in there you can see your breath. Just do it here. I promise I won't look.' He was grinning as he peeled off his sweater, revealing his torso inch by torturous inch.

Shona bit her bottom lip as she watched the skin show. Alasdair wasn't a bit shy about showing off his body, and rightly so. The manual labour he did maintaining the boats and the workout he got from rescuing people was there in every delineated muscle. This wasn't the body of the seventeen-year-old she remembered but of a buff superhero. She could almost picture him now, wearing a second skin of clingy fabric and a cape as he went about the business of saving people's lives. Suddenly she was no longer feeling the cold.

As Alasdair pulled the jumper over his head, she turned away so he wouldn't see her lusty appraisal. With her back to him now, she pulled off her own sodden jumper and wrapped a towel around her top half before she undid her bra. She slipped her arms out of the straps and whipped it off without dislodging the towel. A trick she'd learned as a modest gym goer who wasn't one to prance around the changing rooms stark naked.

She heard the unbuckling of a belt, the pop of buttons on his jeans and imagined him toeing off his boots before they landed with a thud on the hardwood floor. It was hard for her to focus on taking her own clothes off without making a show of herself, thinking about what was going on behind her. The rustle of denim was followed by the clink of his belt buckle hitting the ground, and she just knew if she turned around now he'd be standing naked before her. It was tempting.

Instead she concentrated on drying herself off undercover before deftly replacing the towel with a fresh blanket. She wrapped it around her shoulders, safe in the knowledge her naked body was completely hidden from view.

'Can I turn around yet?' she asked, willing him to have dressed in a similarly modest fashion.

'You can turn around any time you like, but

if you're prudish you might want to wait until I cover up.'

She could hear the laughter in his voice and feel the heat in her cheeks. Both of which made her lash out. 'I am not a prude! Merely respectful of your privacy.'

With that she spun around to make a point, almost disappointed to find he'd wound a towel around his waist.

'We're basically shipwrecked together here, Sho. Privacy is at the bottom of my priority list.'

'Oh? Tell me, what's at the top of that list?' He was being so flirty with her she was becoming increasingly curious about what he had on his mind now they were stranded out here alone.

'Food. I'm starving. Although we should probably try and get these clothes dried off first. I don't want you getting too excited seeing me in nothing but a towel.' The wink he gave her did little to distract her from the short piece of towelling riding low enough on his hips she could see his tan line.

'I think I can manage to control myself,' she said with as much sarcasm as she could muster with the lie she was telling herself.

They pulled over a couple of hardwood chairs from the small table in the corner of the room and draped them with their wet things in front of the fire.

'We've raided Duncan's bedroom and the bathroom. I don't think rummaging in his kitchen cupboard is going to make much more of a difference.'

When he saw Shona's hesitation to follow him towards the kitchen, he added a sweetener. 'I'll replace everything we use tonight. I'm not the thief I was once upon a time.'

'That's not what I was thinking.'

'No? I wouldn't blame you. Although it might give you some idea of the desperation I was in when I did break into people's houses.' He shrugged, and she sensed his earlier bravado leaving him in his slumped shoulders.

She reached out to touch him on the arm. 'Hey. I was always on your side.'

He looked down at her hand on him, covered it with his and lifted it for a kiss. 'Thank you.'

Shona was temporarily speechless from the grateful way he was looking at her and the touch of his lips on her skin. It could have become awkward if the moment had lasted more than a split second, but Alasdair was already back on the hunt for food. She supposed a body like that couldn't live on adrenaline and good will alone.

He was opening and closing the cupboards with both hands, almost frantic now to find something which could pass for dinner. Doing her best to ignore the surge in her blood pressure and the sight of Alasdair's pert behind in that tight towel, Shona assisted him in the search.

'There's milk and butter,' she said peering into the small fridge, which she was pretty sure was only one step up from preserving food in salt as they had in the old days. She prodded at something green and soft in the vegetable drawer but decided not to take any chances and left it where it was.

Alasdair looked into the bread bin. 'We have a loaf which still seems pretty fresh.'

Shona juggled carrying her produce over to the kitchen table whilst still trying to hold on to her blanket shawl, all too aware she was completely naked without it.

'Jackpot!'

Alasdair's outburst almost made her drop everything. 'What?'

He waved a tin of chicken soup at her as though he'd found a winning lottery ticket. 'Tonight, we feast.'

She laughed at his over-the-top excitement for such a little find but that was Alasdair. He was grateful for the smallest things in life and asked for nothing in return. That was why, despite repeatedly telling herself she should stay away from him, she actually enjoyed being with him. Unlike when she'd been with Iain, she didn't have to suppress her own character in order to keep him happy. He'd thanked her for accepting him for who he was without judgement, but really, he'd done the same for her. The longer she spent around him the more she wondered why she continued to resist giving in to the fact that she liked him and wanted them to have more than a working relationship. If only it didn't terrify her so much to even think about getting involved with someone, with him, again.

CHAPTER NINE

ALASDAIR MANAGED TO get the gas stove working to heat up the meagre offerings they'd found in Duncan's supplies. He was definitely going to call in on him at least once a month with more supplies to keep him well stocked up for future emergencies.

After he'd dished the creamy soup into two bowls and buttered some bread, he sat at the small kitchen table with Shona to eat. This day hadn't turned out at all the way he'd planned, but at least they'd got to spend quality time together.

'Does this mean I have to cook for you some time?' Shona clumsily ripped off bits of bread to dip in her soup, with one hand still clutching the blanket for dear life. He wished she would loosen up around him, so he didn't feel like he was on parole. As if one wrong move meant he'd be cast out of her life for a second time.

'Strictly speaking I wouldn't count this as

cooking. Merely reheating. But I wouldn't say no to a dinner invitation. I think that's drinks and a meal you've promised me now.' Okay, there was something of a mixed signal going on here when she looked as though she'd be more comfortable wearing her sodden, skin-clinging clothes. He couldn't fathom why when she was completely covered from the neck down. Unless she thought he had some kind of fetish about her bare feet. Which he didn't. Shona wasn't one to dole out invitations out of social etiquette either. Otherwise half of the island would have been round for dinner at hers at some point over these last months. Whatever the reason, he welcomed the offer of dinner. Preferably somewhere more salubrious than a hermit's cottage. He'd even get someone to cover his shift for him to make sure there were no interruptions next time.

'I think even I could manage something more than tinned soup. Although next time I think we should both be wearing something…more,' she said, flicking a glance at his bare chest.

Alasdair hadn't given his own state of undress much consideration but now he realised that was what she was having more difficulty with. The red stain in her cheeks gave away the path her thoughts were drifting towards. It made him smile to know he was having an effect on her beyond irritation and resignation.

If she'd given him any further indication today that she wanted anything more than this casual working relationship they had he might have acted on it. As it was, she seemed to be fighting the chemistry he knew was there between them with every ounce of willpower. Personally, his reserves were nearly empty. She was the first woman in years who'd made him forget the betrayal he thought he'd never move past. That trust wasn't something he took for granted and meant more to him than sexual attraction.

'If you don't mind my saying, that doesn't look very comfortable or practical. Why don't you wrap it around under your arms and tuck it in? Like a very thick, woollen strapless dress.' He averted his eyes and focused on the few pieces of actual chicken visible in his soup whilst Shona adjusted herself.

'I didn't have you pegged as some sort of fashionista,' she said once she'd sorted herself out and now had two hands free to eat her dinner.

'No? This is a Duncan Laird one-of-a-kind I'm wearing. The fashion-forward citizens of Glasgow would pay a fortune to get their hands on one of these.' He stood up on his chair to display the piece which was temporarily on loan to him.

Shona's eyebrows shot up. 'I'm sure they would.'

In truth the house wasn't warm, but Alasdair would have found an outfit as heavy as Shona's too constricting. Perhaps even a tad chafing with that scratchy wool against his naked body. There could even have been an element of wanting to show off when he knew Shona was appreciating the view. He wasn't blind to the furtive looks, nor was he oblivious to how flustered she was around him at times. Was it so bad to give her a nudge towards admitting she might have feelings for him? He knew he was struggling to continually deny his. Perhaps they'd both been so wounded by the past they were too afraid to be honest about what was happening between them. As far as he could see, they were both enjoying each other's company, and the chemistry between them spoke for itself. He wondered what it was that was really scaring them about the idea of being together. And if either of them was brave enough to front it out.

After their so-called dinner they washed up the few dirty dishes and retired to the warmth of the living room. There was one battered, wing-backed armchair and a small, threadbare moss-green settee to sit on. Alasdair waited for Shona to choose her seat, glad when she settled on the settee, leaving him the armchair.

'I'm afraid there's no television.' There was nothing in the room to provide any distraction, and he was sure Shona would have preferred some sort of buffer between them.

'I see that. I wonder what he does for entertainment or fun out here?' She looked around but there were no obvious signs of the modern-day technology most people took for granted in their leisure time.

'He's pretty self-sufficient, so maybe he doesn't have a lot of time for anything else.' There would always be the livestock to sort out and maintaining whatever crops Duncan grew in order to survive.

'There's a radio and quite a few books, I suppose. Very back-to-basics.'

'Not a bad thing. He could probably make a fortune renting this place out as a retreat for busy city workers who need to unplug themselves from the digital age for a while.'

'Braelin's a bit like that, haven't you found? There's a different pace of life on the island from the mainland. Was that part of the attraction for you coming back?' Shona curled up on the sofa, seemingly more at ease now there was a bit of space between them. She had some reason to be wary of him when she looked so delectable wearing nothing but an old blanket. It was easy to imagine her like this lying in his bed, shoulders bare and hair loose, tumbling over her naked skin.

He had to blink away the images of her caught up in his rumpled sheets to answer her coherently. 'I hadn't really thought of it that way, but yeah, there are elements of that, I guess. I mean, I'm always busy here too but there's something more personal about living on the island compared to a big city.'

'You get lost among the crowd in a city,' she offered.

'Yes. Exactly that. Despite my past record and the relationship with my father, I'm sure if I'd been here when my ex tore my life apart I would've had some sort of support from the community to get me back on my feet. Perhaps, deep down, I knew that. Otherwise, why would I have worked so hard to change everyone's opinion of me?' Those days after his future as a father had been taken away from him had been the darkest of his life. That was saying something after the upbringing he'd had.

Friends at work, passing acquaintances, hadn't been the same as the people he'd known on the island, or at least the one person who'd been there for him when he'd needed it the most. He looked at Shona, who was listening intently, and he knew she was waiting for an opening to assure him he had people around him now who cared. Shona was the only person who'd ever showed him unconditional love and he'd thrown it away. Perhaps, subconsciously, part of the reason he'd come back was because he wanted her in his life again to talk to, to give him hope.

'I think when our lives were upended we both craved something familiar. That was Braelin. We came back here like wounded animals, wanting to keep ourselves safe somewhere.' Hurt glistened in Shona's eyes and it was clear she'd been through a tough time too before deciding to make the change. Alasdair knew from experience what a big step it was to give up everything you'd called home for most of your adult life and risk coming back, and he knew the trauma that caused it. He was sorry she'd had to experience it, albeit in different circumstances.

'And do you? Feel safe? I wonder, because sometimes, Shona, you seem so on edge around me.' He didn't know the ins and outs of her marriage or what she'd been through this past year as a widow, but if he was what made her so uncomfortable, he would back off if she asked. As much as he wanted to be with her, it wouldn't be at the expense of her peace of mind.

She swung her legs around until she was sitting on the edge of her seat, hands clasped in her lap. 'I did…until I saw you again.'

His heart plummeted. He was the cause of her discomfort. When he thought they'd been flirting and dancing around their attraction, he'd completely misread the situation. 'I'm so sorry. I never meant to upset you.'

Alasdair got up, deciding to put his clothes on, wet or not, rather than continue feeding her discomfort.

Shona got on her feet as he moved the chairs away from the front of the fire and began gathering up his clothes. 'You didn't.'

'You just said you don't feel safe around me and here we are, half naked and stranded in a cottage. It's enough to cause you to have a full panic attack and I'm parading around in nothing but a towel.' He was the lowest of the low, focusing on his own needs and wants rather than considering how Shona was feeling. Especially when she'd already shot down any attempt to capitalise on her brief lapse of judgement in the car the other day.

He began fussing with his clothes, preparing to cover up and put some sort of barrier between them. Apparently, Shona had other ideas. She pressed the palm of her hand firmly against his chest. 'Don't.'

'Don't what? Be honest about what's happening here? One of us has to be. There's no point in trying to save my feelings at the cost of yours. I'll get dressed and sleep in the other room. I'll take you back to Braelin first thing and you'll never have to see me again if that's what you want.' It would kill him, as it had done when he'd ended their fledgling relationship all of those years ago, but he'd do it for her sake.

She didn't move her hand. 'That's not what I want.'

Alasdair was afraid to jump to conclusions about what it was she did want, and needed her to spell it out to him so he didn't make any more mistakes where Shona was concerned. He'd hurt her enough for one lifetime. 'Then talk to me. Tell me how I make you uncomfortable and I'll stop whatever it is.'

'It's nothing you've done. Believe me, it's not your fault.'

He saw her swallow, building up the courage to say what was holding her back, keeping her frightened.

Alasdair knew when to keep quiet and let the lady have the floor.

Shona was having palpitations as she prepared to come clean about why she was so hot and cold around Alasdair. It wasn't helping that she could feel those taut muscles of his chest at her fingertips. She supposed it would be completely out of order to stroke that warm, smooth skin until she confessed her feelings for him.

'I'm afraid of myself. Of how I feel around you. I—I don't want to get hurt again, Alasdair.' Despite her attempt at being strong, standing up and being honest rather than letting Alasdair blame himself for her erratic behaviour, her voice cracked a little. A sign that the pain of losing people in her life was never far from the surface. It was difficult for her to believe that giving in to temptation with Alasdair would lead to anything other than heartache when experience had taught her otherwise.

'I would never, ever do anything to cause you pain. Surely you know that by now?' His knitted brow expressed confusion that she could doubt his intentions after explaining his past behaviour and the two of them getting to know each other again.

'Not intentionally, but I've lost too many people close to me. I'm afraid of falling for you and something bad happening. I can't get past the danger you face out at sea with every call-out. I'm just scared, Alasdair.'

His forehead evened out into a smile. 'You trust me, though?'

She nodded. It would be pointless to deny it because she wouldn't even have set foot in the boat if she didn't believe he would look out for her.

'Then trust I can take care of myself, that I can do my job well enough not to get killed.' He covered her hand with his and lifted it to his mouth for a kiss just as he'd done earlier. A gesture so sweet it would never fail to make her smile. 'So, with my promise not to die any time soon in mind, tell me what it is you want, Shona?'

His eyes darkened as he moved in closer to her, his lips almost touching hers, asking permission for more. She knew he was making fun about her fears a little bit but there was truth in what he was saying too. These past few days she'd witnessed him in his working environment and he was confident and capable. There had been no reason to believe he'd do anything to put himself at more risk than the next person.

Being confronted like this, having to face the fact it was her own fears preventing her from enjoying life, it seemed like self-sabotage to continue denying her feelings. And now he was so concerned about her welfare she was sure she could trust him with her heart. It was about time she threw off the shackles she'd imposed upon herself and truly tasted freedom without fear.

She wet her dry lips with her tongue so she could answer him clearly. 'You.'

Her pulse was galloping with the wait for his response. She was leaving herself vulnerable here, exposing her feelings and opening up her heart to make room for him. He could crush her completely with a rejection now, but it was apparently the green light Alasdair had been waiting for.

His eyes didn't leave her lips as he reached out and pulled her towards him. She went willingly to meet him; her mouth mashed against his, desperate to unleash the desire bubbling up inside her.

Shona caught his head between her hands, holding him right where she wanted him. His arms were wrapped tightly around her too, locking their bodies tight together. The blanket seemed bulkier now, inconvenient, when she couldn't feel his naked skin against hers. Even if it was a one-time deal, she wanted all of him tonight. They'd come so close in the past it would be cruel for her to miss out on exploring their passion to its fullest yet again. Isolated as they were from the real world, and with Alasdair's kisses more scorching than the heat from the fire, the next step seemed inevitable. Here, there were no obstacles.

Shona hadn't been with anyone since Iain. Or before him. Alasdair had shown her today she could trust him. He'd had her life, and Duncan's, in his hands and they'd survived. So far.

Alas, her stomach was doing gymnastics at the thought of getting to know someone else's body, of Alasdair exploring hers. This time it was borne of excitement and anticipation rather than through fear. They were no longer horny, inexperienced teenagers worried about reputation or rejection. Well, apparently still horny, but now they were adults, going into this with their eyes wide open.

She didn't want to feel as though this was her first time all over again. Needed some way of proving to herself she was ready for this. That she was fully aware of what she was doing. Gradually she weaned herself away from Alasdair's lips, finding satisfaction in the glazed look in his eyes as she took a step back out of his embrace.

'What's wrong?' he asked, his voice husky and clearly not ready for the kissing to cease.

'Nothing. I was just feeling a little…' she opened the blanket and let it fall to her feet '…hot.'

Now she was actually standing naked in front of him she realised she was more vulnerable than ever. This was it. She was offering him everything, and if he turned her down again she'd never recover from the ultimate humiliation.

The longer he took to respond, the more she was tempted to grab the closest thing to cover herself up. She could hardly look at him now in case she saw disappointment or embarrassment clouding his face. A second before she was about to strategically cover the bits of her that were going to remain completely private from now on, Alasdair made a guttural sound of appreciation.

'Yes. Yes, you are.'

She let out a little squeal of delight as he advanced on her with devilish intent.

The kissing began again in earnest. That hard, breath-stealing kind of wanting one another which left her bruised when it stopped. Before she could protest his lips were on her again, at her throat, on her breast. He took her firmly in his hand and ran his tongue over her nipple, teasing it into a tight peak. The sharp graze of his teeth over the sensitive tip made her suck in a breath. There was the small possibility he'd hurt her, but she trusted he intended only pleasure. Something he proved to be true when he suckled and squeezed her breast until arousal flooded every part of her body.

Alasdair continued on his quest to fulfil her

every need, tickling her belly with his stubble as he moved down her body, kissing and licking a sensual path to where she was aching most for him.

On his knees now, hands at her hips, he teased her thighs apart. Eyes closed, ready for everything he wanted to give her, Shona sucked in a ragged breath. That first lap of his tongue was nearly her undoing, then he ventured deep inside and she had to steady herself on his shoulders before she collapsed.

She could hear her own moans of pleasure somewhere out there, beyond all those sensations taking her to a higher plane, but she was powerless to quieten them. Completely at Alasdair's mercy.

It wasn't long before that swell of ecstasy became overwhelming. Too much for her to hold back even if she'd wanted to. Alasdair brought her to climax at the tip of his tongue and didn't relent until every shudder and tremor of her orgasm had subsided.

She came down to join him on the fireside rug and kissed him with gratitude, tasting herself on his lips. There were no words needed as he laid her down and removed the towel from around his waist, the last obstacle between their bodies. The head of his proud erection slid into her slick, wet opening without hesitation. Shona gasped as he filled her so completely she had to ask him to wait until her body adjusted to him.

Alasdair took his time helping her to relax with his languid kisses, and whispered sweet nothings, telling her how beautiful she was. When he moved inside her he was slow at first, letting her feel the full length of him as he withdrew, before forging their bodies back together.

'Is this going to last?' she had to ask when she was falling for him more with every kiss, every moment they spent in each other's arms. This was everything she could have wished for, but that was what frightened her. The joy she was experiencing with him now meant the greater the heartbreak if it was all to go wrong.

'I'm doing my best,' he said with a grin, deliberately misunderstanding her and making her chuckle.

'You know what I mean.'

'Can we talk about this later, Sho? I'm trying to focus on something else here.' She could feel Alasdair smile against her neck while he was kissing her and trying to distract her. They couldn't avoid the subject of what happened when they went back to Braelin and reality for ever. Except he was lifting her legs up onto his shoulders and...

Oh, that feels good.

* * *

Alasdair was literally in heaven. Who would have thought he'd find peace in a remote cottage with the first girl who'd ever captured his heart?

He knew Shona had questions but he didn't have the answers because he didn't want to think about tomorrow. Only now. All the fears about what could happen or who might hurt whom could wait. He wanted to enjoy just one night without thinking about the past or things neither of them could change. One night just feeling…fantastic.

It had been a while for both of them, yet they fitted together so perfectly it was as if they were made to be together. She'd surprised him when she'd purposely dropped her blanket. The bold move had prompted the last thread of his restraint to snap. He'd wanted her for so long this seemed like a beautiful, erotic dream he never wanted to end.

Despite the lack of amenities on the island, he'd happily stay here with Shona for ever. Preferably naked. She was even more stunning than he'd imagined under that blanket and that cute elf outfit. Beautiful, sexy, and his for tonight.

She'd been waiting for this as long as he had. He could tell when she was so receptive, so eager, so wet for him. Alasdair tensed, wanting to prolong his pleasure as much as possible, at the same time watching Shona's. It was a powerful aphrodisiac seeing her writhing in ecstasy beneath him, knowing he was the one who was making her feel that way—out of control, abandoned to desire and free from whatever it was that usually kept her so guarded.

She tightened around him, causing him to groan as he clung to the last of his control. Her breathing was coming in short vocal bursts, getting quicker with each thrust inside her. Faster and faster he took her, driving her towards the edge, wanting to see her fall into that blissful abyss once more. Wanting to be there with her at the last push. As she wrapped her arms and legs around him, dug her heels in and rode him hard, Alasdair was lost. The roar of absolute satisfaction he gave was ripped from deep inside his soul. It was the culmination of his pent-up longing for this woman finally being released into her warm, wet body.

Shona's high-pitched moan, along with her arousal washing over them both, heralded her final climax, sending tremor after tremor coursing through Alasdair once more. When their bodies finally stilled, he was sure he'd never see or walk again, he was so thoroughly depleted.

As he pulled the blanket over their bodies to keep them warm for the night, he knew he wanted this to last. Possibly for ever.

CHAPTER TEN

SHONA WOKE UP with Alasdair's arms around her and his body spooned against hers. It was an extremely pleasant way to wake up. They must have dozed off shortly after their explosive love-making and slept right through the night. Being stranded here hadn't turned out to be as bad as she'd first imagined. In fact, it had become a fantasy island, where all her X-rated thoughts about the man beside her had come true.

She snuggled back against him with a smug grin, thoroughly satisfied with herself and everything she'd shared with Alasdair last night. He nuzzled into her neck and tightened his hold on her.

'Morning,' he mumbled into her ear, sending little shivers over her skin, despite the blanket and the fire keeping them warm.

'Morning. We must have tired ourselves out last night.'

'Hmm-mm. Well, today is another day and

I'm awake.' He kissed her neck and made sure her body was thoroughly awakened too.

'I can tell,' she said as his hardness pressed into the small of her back. She was tempted to turn around and face him except his hands were wandering over her body, remapping everywhere they'd been last night and everywhere she wanted them again.

Alasdair slipped his hands between her thighs and tested her readiness with his fingers. 'Apparently someone else is raring to go too.'

She couldn't argue or get embarrassed when the evidence was there of her increasing arousal. It was enough to fuel his own desire as he pushed himself up behind her. Shona wasn't ready for this romantic fantasy to end just yet. Especially when he made her feel so good and reignited the passion of their youth by a hundredfold. She moved back against him and Alasdair accepted the invitation.

He entered her slowly and she sighed with contentment. If only they could wake up like this every morning she'd be an even happier woman. Weighing up a life without him so she didn't get hurt, versus how she felt when she was with him, seemed like a no-brainer. She was so happy with Alasdair it was apparent what she'd been missing out on all this time. Passion, excitement and perhaps even another chance at love. It was a big jump for her to consider getting into another relationship, but here, so far away from her fears of losing someone she loved, she could believe it was possible. It was a very lovely dream which was heating up by the second.

This time when they made love there was something deeper between them. A familiarity with each other's bodies already, which only heightened the amazing sensations he created within her. It was going to be harder than ever returning to Braelin, waking up alone in bed and knowing what she'd be giving up just to protect her fragile heart.

For now, they were making the most of their isolation and the feeling of being the only two people in the world. In some ways it was like that summer they'd had together. Alone with him, making out on the beach, she'd never been so happy, but once they'd gone back to school and normality, everything had fallen apart. She'd been bitten once too often to believe in happy endings. Although Alasdair was gradually making her want to think they still existed.

It was the cold which stirred Alasdair from his slumber. The heat from Shona's naked body was no longer keeping him warm, his arms were empty, and the fire almost out. He didn't panic, knowing there was nowhere she could have run off to if she'd had second thoughts about what they'd got up to last night. Certainly, she'd seemed more than satisfied when they'd repeated the experience this morning.

He didn't know what the future held for them as a couple, if anything, but it was clear they had feelings for one another. She'd shown faith in his abilities yesterday on the boat and she'd trusted him last night with her heart and her body. Steps she wouldn't have taken if she didn't believe in him or want to be with him. Things that meant a great deal to Alasdair, given his wariness about opening his life up to include someone else again. He knew he was falling for her when he thought about her all the time and wanted to spend every spare minute he had with her. Shona wasn't the sort of woman to sleep with him simply because of convenience's sake or a base need for physical release. There was more to this than sleeping together to get closure on their past too. If they would actually admit that to each other they might stand a chance together. He for one was willing to try.

The living room door opened and Shona peered in. 'I'm making some tea if you want some before we head off?'

'Yes, please. I see you're dressed already,' he noted with disappointment. It seemed as though she was keen to get off the island as soon as possible, when he'd have happily spent another day lying here making love with her.

'I took advantage of the hot water and peace and quiet for a long soak in the bath. I love my nieces to bits but it's impossible to do that at Chrissie's.'

'You should've said and I would have happily joined you.'

'I'm sure you would but there was a reason I needed to soothe my aching body.' The colour rose in her freshly scrubbed face and Alasdair knew exactly what she was talking about. There were parts of him which hadn't had such an extensive workout in so long they were feeling the after-effects too. Not that it would put him off doing it all again. He didn't think he could ever have too much of Shona and hoped that after some R&R she'd think the same way.

She disappeared into the kitchen and he followed like a faithful hound who suddenly couldn't imagine life without her. It was as if those intervening years had never happened and they'd picked up from where they'd left off on the beach all that time ago. Moving on from their teenage hormones and angst to the idea of a fully-fledged adult relationship complete with complex emotions was a scary prospect but exciting at the same time. Shona wasn't a completely unknown entity to him and didn't come with all the fearful attachments a new love interest would bring him. He knew her background, her relationship history and her own anxieties. She'd been so open with him he couldn't imagine her ever wanting to hurt him or anyone else. Shona had never been someone he could easily forget, and, now he was also aware of how amazing together they were in bed—or in this case, on the floor—it would be impossible.

'We're not in any rush to go home, are we? I mean, neither of us has work today.' Alasdair slid his arms around Shona's waist as she stood at the kitchen worktop, making the tea. He rested his head on her shoulder in a puppy dog plea for more attention.

'I'm not sure it would be fair of us to take more advantage of Mr Laird's home than we already have. I phoned the hospital when I woke; Duncan had a comfortable night and will probably be home soon.' She finished pouring the hot water into the cups and leaned back into his embrace.

Alasdair had worried she'd changed her mind about wanting to be with him when he'd woken to find her gone, but such a subtle movement told him he was wrong. It would be an imposition to continue to use Duncan's cottage for their liaisons now the danger outside had passed. The weather seemed a lot calmer this morning and really, other than his libido, there was no reason for them to be trespassing here. However, that didn't equate to him being willing to go straight back to Braelin, where there was a chance they'd carry on as though the greatest night of his life had never happened. Shona was so skittish about the idea of a relationship with him he was sure she'd find the first excuse to call things off before they really got going. He was determined to do his best not to let that happen.

'We could always go ahead with the trip we'd originally planned.'

'What? Going to Glasgow?' Shona spun around in his arms to face him. Thankfully, she wasn't immediately shooting down the idea. It gave him some hope of having another day with her.

'Why not? It's nice outside. If we leave now we could get there by lunchtime. How about it? Santa and his Chief Elf could really make a day of it in the big smoke.' The more he thought about it, the more he liked the idea. It could be their first official date as a couple if the notion didn't completely freak Shona out. A little shopping, some lunch and time together sounded like the perfect afternoon to him. If he wasn't allowed to spend it with her in bed...

'I'll have to let Chrissie know in case she wonders where I am, but yeah, that sounds fun.' She was smiling as she circled her arms around his neck and gave him a kiss on the lips.

Yes, Alasdair was going to make this the best Winter Wonderland promo/first date ever and prove to Shona he was worth giving a second chance.

The sail to the mainland was a lot smoother than it had been the previous day. Much to Shona's relief. They cleaned up the cottage and left a note for Mr Laird explaining why they'd had to shelter at his place for the night and promising to replace everything they'd used. Her conscience was eased a little more when Alasdair spoke to the nephew on the phone and explained the circumstances. He was only too pleased they'd been there to assist his uncle and dismissed any concerns about their having trespassed on the property.

It took a busy train ride to get to Glasgow city centre and they changed into their costumes in the shopping centre toilets across from the station.

'I think we're causing a bit of a stir,' Shona said as she joined Alasdair out on the steps leading to Buchanan Street, the main shopping thoroughfare. Adults and children alike were stopping to stare. Unsurprising, given their outfits, but not something she was used to.

'That's the idea. Hopefully we'll drum up a lot of interest in the Winter Wonderland and increase our visitor numbers this year. It would look good for the reigning Santa and Chief Elf. Speaking of which, have I told you how cute you are? Although I am beginning to miss the blanket dress...'

Shona hit him with the bundle of flyers in her hands even though she couldn't wipe the smile off her face at the compliment and reminder of their recent antics. 'Focus, Santa. We have important work to do today.'

'But we still get to play later, right?' He was standing much too close, his voice way too loaded with suggestion, for her to remain unaffected by him. Despite the fat suit and beard. Those eyes, so dark with undisguised desire, were enough to make a girl swoon. The quicker they did what they were here for so they could 'play', the better. Not that she was going to make it easy for him. She liked being the target of his affections, in every way possible.

'We'll see,' she said casually, before spinning away on the heel of her elf shoe.

Santa gave an uncharacteristic growl before bouncing down the steps after her.

'Come to Braelin Island for our Winter Wonderland. Sample the local produce, visit our Christmas fair and take part in our candlelit carol service.' Shona was getting into the swing of things now, handing out information leaflets to passing shoppers. Alasdair, of course, had his own spin on things, ringing a bell to get people's attention, taking selfies with anyone who looked game and taking names for his naughty or nice lists. People loved him.

She had to tear her gaze away when he bent down to talk to a child in a buggy, listening intently to the boy's extensive toy requests for the big day. She thought again that he would have made a wonderful father, and she was angry on his behalf that the opportunity had been taken from him so cruelly. She liked to think she'd have made a good mother too, but that was on her and her past impetuous behaviour. These days she was more careful about the decisions she made. Which was why it had taken her so long to give in to the obvious feelings and attraction towards this man. Only time would tell what would happen once they took off their costumes and returned to reality. For now, though, she was willing to go with her gut feeling that they could have something special if she stopped holding back the way she'd done last night.

With the winter well and truly underway, it began to get dark late afternoon, but the Christmas lights and music from nearby buskers made for a very festive atmosphere. Shona was pleasantly surprised by the reception they were given by most people already in the Christmas mood. Although she was beginning to feel the cold on her bare thighs, and she was sure her nose was the same colour as her rouged cheeks.

'Why don't we take a break and go and get warmed up?' Alasdair suggested, either feeling the cold himself or taking pity on her.

'Where are we going to go dressed like this?' As much as she'd love to sit by a warm fire somewhere, she didn't relish the idea of waltzing into a restaurant full of people on Christmas outings, dressed as an elf.

'I know just the place,' he declared, linking his arm through hers before skipping his way down the street. Shona had no choice but to do the same or be left behind. She didn't care who was looking or laughing when she was positively giddy with feel-good endorphins. At this point in time she'd happily run away with Mr Alasdair Murray to anywhere he wanted. After the year she'd had of loss, grief and fear of the unknown, he was a much-needed breath of fresh air blowing the dust from her staid life. She'd come to Braelin not knowing what her future held, but now she was hoping he'd be a part of it.

When she thought she couldn't run any more, the twinkling lights and hubbub of the Christmas market came into view, completing the magical afternoon. Familiar Christmas tunes played out over the speakers, and little wooden chalets were displaying their wares of handicrafts and home-baked goods. The air was full of cinnamon and other spices and smelled like Christmas heaven.

'It's so long since I've been to a Christmas market. I missed pottering about last year. There didn't seem any point in it. Now I wish Chrissie and the girls were here to see it too.' The catch in her voice was unexpected as the emotions of the season took over. It was the juxtaposition of loss combined with the joy of reconnecting with her family that suddenly overwhelmed her. As though she should feel guilty on all counts by being here enjoying herself.

Alasdair took her hands and warmed them between his. 'Ours is better, and you'll get to experience it with your family this year. No time for shopping, I'm afraid. This visit is strictly for reheating purposes only.'

He strode into the busy market, keeping hold

of her hand as he made a path through the stall-browsing public until they arrived at the largest wooden building in the square.

Inside was a full-length bar crammed with partygoers and office workers on their annual outing, complete with flashing reindeer antlers and festive sweaters. 'A pub? What about getting back home?'

Whilst the idea of spending another night offshore with Alasdair was appealing, she had work and family to get back to. She hoped she wasn't bringing out the irresponsible side in him the way he was helping her recapture the fun in life. It could have repercussions for him too if he started ditching work the way he'd done with school.

'Don't worry, I'm not sailing back drunk. Even Santa indulges in a little mulled wine to warm his insides on a cold winter's night.' He mistook her concerns for a different one about her personal safety, making her slightly uncomfortable that her thoughts had even drifted that way. She'd gone sex mad!

'Okay…if you're sure.'

'There's a space over there by the heater. Go and warm yourself up and I'll get the drinks in.' He was being the gentleman in ensuring her comfort and at the same time detracting attention from her by presenting Santa at the packed bar.

She tried to make herself as small as possible in the corner in case any of the inebriated crowd decided to come and make conversation. Meanwhile most of them were congregating around Alasdair, slapping him on the back and offering to buy him drinks. All of which he declined politely to order his own. He made his way back carrying two small cups of mulled wine as his new friends sang tuneless Christmas songs to accompany him. Eventually they lost interest in anything other than trying to out-sing each other in a drink-fuelled karaoke session.

'These are on the house, apparently.' He had to shout above the noise so she could hear him. 'The barman says we're the only ones who seem to be actually working today. I've left a pile of leaflets on the counter too, which might drum up some more visitors.'

'Thanks.' Shona wrapped her hands around the cup, thankful for the heat, and inhaled the steam swirling up from the wine. The scent of orange and cloves warmed her insides just as much. Everything Christmas was right there in her hands, and when she sipped the hot beverage she closed her eyes in ecstasy.

'You're enjoying that a bit too much,' Alasdair laughed as he sipped his own mulled wine.

'Isn't it just the best, though? Mum used to make it on Christmas Eve, non-alcoholic for the kids of course. The smell used to permeate the whole house, so it was still in the air when we woke up on Christmas morning to open our presents. It just brings back such happy memories for me.'

'It tastes good,' Alasdair agreed, once he'd pulled off his beard to taste the wine. When he saw her roll her eyes at his lack of sufficient enthusiasm, he added, 'What? It's all I got.' He smiled but again she was reminded that he didn't have any relatable Christmas stories. She thought it was about time he made some new memories to replace the sadness of past Christmases the way he was encouraging her to do.

'You should come to ours for Christmas,' she said without thinking. It was her natural response to someone she knew would be alone for the holidays when she had family and Christmas spirit in abundance. She simply hadn't thought through the consequences of any of it when she hadn't asked Chrissie or considered what it would mean to her and Alasdair. It was a big step to spend Christmas together when they hadn't really discussed the nature of their relationship yet. One which she really should have slept on. Alone.

'Really?' Alasdair nearly choked on his drink. 'You wouldn't mind?'

It wasn't as if she could retract the invitation now it had been issued. Besides, he seemed so genuinely thrilled at the idea Shona wouldn't want to disappoint him. They'd also slept together, so coming over for dinner shouldn't be a bigger deal than that.

'Of course not. There'll be plenty of mulled wine and turkey to go around. You could even come over on Christmas Eve if you're free? I'm sure we could use a hand building some of the many playsets Chrissie has been stockpiling for the twins.'

'I could even dress for the occasion if it's called for.' He patted his false belly, but Shona much preferred him *sans* fat suit—or any clothes, really. She took another sip of wine, hoping it would explain an extra rosy glow to her complexion at the thought.

'Don't worry, you can have the night off and enjoy yourself with no expectations.' Although she was wondering if it would make more sense for him to sleep over and, if so, how on earth she'd explain that to the other members of the household.

'Fingers crossed. I'll still be on call for the lifeboat. It wouldn't be right to ask someone to cover for me when the rest of the guys all have families.'

'That doesn't seem fair.'

'It's the nature of the job. You should know that.'

She did. There was no Christmas break for the emergency services. Someone had to cover all the holidays.

Alasdair was also reminding her that he had a job beyond the jolly Santa Claus he was currently playing. Being on the lifeboat was part of him and it wasn't fair of her to continue making him feel bad about it. Even if her anxiety was threatening to resurface the closer they got to returning home.

The drunken office workers at the bar launched into bursts of jeering and singing as they pogo-danced with their arms around each other, occasionally straying over the line and bumping into Shona and Alasdair's table.

'Go easy, mate,' Alasdair warned one sweaty-backed dancer who knocked against Shona and spilled her wine over her lap.

The territorial display was enough for the man to back off, mumbling an apology to the miffed Santa, who was on his feet ready to defend his elf's honour. It was quite sweet to have him looking out for her, even if she was capable of looking after herself. She imagined he would have done the same for anyone wronged, but it was a long time since she'd had anyone being protective over her. It was nice to know she had someone looking out for her and she wasn't completely on her own anymore.

Once trouble was averted Alasdair sat down again and she flashed him a grateful smile. 'I think they've had more than one glass of mulled wine.'

'Yeah, we should probably go before they get too much more lairy. We're sitting ducks dressed like this.'

'You're just afraid they'll end up on your lap, telling you what they want for Christmas.'

'Of course I am. Do you fancy telling that lot all they're getting is coal in their stockings this year?' He grinned as he sank the rest of his wine.

'No, thanks. I'm just the helper, not the main man.' Shona finished her drink too, the tangy taste of cloves and red wine only adding to the warm feeling Alasdair had already created inside her. These past twenty-four hours in his company had been anything but boring. Discovering as much about herself and her likes as she had about him. She was keen to carry on exploring both under normal conditions at home, to see if this thing between them had been a fluke or could be sustainable away from fantasy land.

Just as they were ready to leave, the bloke who'd bumped into Shona earlier decided a dance routine was needed to accompany the singing. He climbed up onto a small round table which wobbled precariously as he kicked his legs up whilst still swilling from his pint glass.

The clattering sound followed by a glass smashing came as no surprise, but when Shona turned back to see the aftermath, the amount of blood seeping across the wooden floor did shock her.

'Alasdair.' She tugged on his coat sleeve to pull him back, knowing their help was going to be needed in a different capacity this afternoon. She was never truly off the clock either.

The singing had stopped now, replaced by lots of shouting. Mainly from the man who'd fallen. His friends were standing around holding their heads in their hands and not doing anything terribly useful.

'Phone an ambulance,' Alasdair shouted to the barman who, apart from Shona, was probably the only other sober person in the room. Then he manhandled the crowd out of the way so they could get to the injured party on the floor.

'I'm a nurse and he's a paramedic,' Shona explained, following his lead.

They kneeled at either side of the patient to

assess his injuries. It was the broken glass which had done the damage more than the fall. Given the waft of alcohol coming from his breath, she was sure he hadn't felt either. Especially when he was still trying to get up.

'Where's ma beer?'

'In a puddle on the floor around you. Now, stay still; you've got some broken glass stuck in you.' Alasdair lifted the hand which had been holding the pint glass and was now bleeding profusely.

The barman rushed over, bringing the obligatory first-aid kit, as well as a dustpan and brush to sweep up the remnants of glass. 'The ambulance is on its way.'

'Good. I'm just going to clean the hand and get as much glass as I can out of the wound.' Alasdair picked out the biggest shards which were embedded into the skin and dropped them into the dustpan out of the way.

Shona took out the contents of the first-aid box and cleaned and dressed the area, but she wasn't convinced that was the source of all the blood. She opened his shirt to check for any other visible signs of injury.

She rolled him onto his side and saw the tell-tale scarlet stain spreading over his shirt. 'Alasdair…'

He came around to her side and carefully

lifted the shirt up to expose the site. Those around them echoed his sharp intake of breath. A large piece of glass had pierced the shirt fabric and was protruding from the man's side. It was possible he'd landed on it during his fall.

'What? What is it?' Their patient was twisting his body, trying to see for himself.

'There's some more glass. We need you to stay still so we can remove it without causing you any further damage.' Shona was glad he had anaesthetised himself with alcohol so it wouldn't be so painful when they did pull out the glass. She was sure she and Alasdair had seen enough drunken injuries like this one to know it wasn't deep enough to likely have caused any serious tissue or muscle damage.

'Deep breaths,' Alasdair advised. 'In. Out. In...' He pulled the shard out on the last exhale, prompting a melodramatic squeal from the injured party.

The bleeding began in earnest again and Shona moved quickly to stem the flow with a wad of cotton gauze and placed a dressing over the site. 'You're probably going to need some stitches at the hospital, and you should get checked over for any signs of concussion.' Although how they'd be able to tell that from his drunken haze she wasn't sure.

The sound of sirens could be heard not too far

away, and Shona knew it was time to hand over responsibility to the medical team who were actually on duty today. The paramedics came in carrying their equipment and she left Alasdair to give them the lowdown whilst she kept their patient still. The team could decide whether or not they wanted to use a neck brace after the fall he'd had.

'Thanks for your help but we'll take over from here,' the older paramedic insisted when they approached.

'No problem.' This was one occasion she was happy to let someone else take over. It had been a long couple of days and she wasn't exactly dressed to be taken seriously. A point proved when she and Alasdair were ready to leave and another chorus of Christmas songs serenaded them out of the door.

He took it in good humour, putting his beard back on and waving, before giving them one last, 'Ho, ho, ho.'

'Do you think we can call it a day? All the excitement has worn me out.' She stifled a yawn as she waved goodbye to their admiring crowd.

'Definitely. We should get back before it gets any darker. I think we've done more than enough work promoting ourselves and Braelin.'

'I had fun too,' she added, so he didn't think it had all been too much for her. They'd had a good time together since the moment they'd woken up in one another's arms that morning. The medical drama had simply drained what was left of her energy after spending the afternoon on her feet chatting to potential visitors. What she wouldn't give for them to be wrapped up again in front of a fire. On their own. She doubted they'd get much of a chance to repeat last night once she was back living with her sister and nieces.

CHAPTER ELEVEN

THE TRIP BACK to Braelin was more relaxed than the first one Shona and Alasdair had undertaken. They'd changed back into their own clothes before boarding the boat again to regain some sense of normality. The peace and solitude as they sailed was lovely. Especially when it was interspersed with lots of handholding, embracing and long, leisurely smooches. If it hadn't been for the incident in the beer garden, she would have called it the perfect day.

By the time they reached the island it was dark, and Shona knew she had to check in with Chrissie after being gone for so long. As much as she loved being with her family, she considered what it would be like having a place of her own where she wasn't expected to account for her whereabouts and had some privacy. Enabling her to have a personal life.

She waited on the jetty while Alasdair tied

up the boat securely for the night, sad that their time together had to come to an end for now.

'I should get back and face the inquisition,' she told him once he came to join her on the walkway.

'That's one good thing about not having anyone to go home to,' he said, pulling her into another embrace.

'Don't get me wrong, I love Chrissie to bits, but some things I want to keep private.' She was toying with the zipper on his jacket, memories of him wearing a lot less coming to mind. Last night was theirs, and she didn't want to share it with anyone else.

'You could always just call in to collect a few things and come and stay at mine. Then there's no time for lengthy explanations about what you got up to last night and this morning.' He was teasing her about their wanton behaviour, but it was a tempting offer.

She toyed with the suggestion and all it entailed. More of Alasdair. More of last night. At this moment in time it was all she wanted.

When had he become her whole world?

Perhaps she needed a time out after all when her thoughts were revolving entirely around him. Some space to think logically about what she was getting into mightn't be such a bad thing. It was important she was able to determine the difference between the euphoria of a budding romance and falling in love with someone. She was afraid it had been so long since she'd experienced either of those two things that she was confusing one for the other. Talking to Chrissie would probably help get some perspective on that too. She didn't have to go into details. No matter how hard she was pushed to give them.

Alasdair insisted on walking Shona home. Partly for her safety, partly out of good manners, and partly because he wanted to extend what time they had left together. There was always the chance she'd change her mind about wanting to be with him once she'd had time to think it over properly. He'd do anything to make her hang on to the special memories they had of being stranded in that cottage together last night.

He pulled the collar of her coat up around her neck then used it to pull her in for a kiss. A hard, passionate, don't-you-forget-what-we-have-together smooch that left her dazed on her doorstep. 'We may as well give your sister something to gawp at.'

'Is that the only reason you're kissing me?' Shona asked, a little breathlessly. They'd both clocked Chrissie at the window, peeking out from behind the curtains, when they'd walked up the path.

'I don't need a reason or an audience.' To prove it he backed her into the porch, against the wall and away from prying eyes. He cupped her face in his hands and pressed his lips firmly against hers, branding her with his mouth and making her his. The only regret he had was that he would have to stop kissing her and go home alone to his bed.

He never dared believe he'd find anyone he'd want to share his life with again, but these past days with Shona had made him think differently. It wasn't just the sex, although that had been mind-blowing, and he was keen to carry on from where they'd left off this morning. From where this kiss would have led if she came home with him. No, it was everything about being with Shona which made him want more of her in his life.

The strength she'd shown today and yesterday when dealing with the injured was an insight into the woman she'd become. The kind, warm-hearted girl he'd fallen for that summer was still very much there inside her, caring and full of fun. He was prepared to wait until she was ready to commit to something more than one night, willing to gamble his heart again if it meant they could be together further down the line. After all, he'd waited years just to be with her here again.

'Okay. Point proven,' she conceded when they finally stopped for breath.

'When can I see you again?'

'I don't know... I'll have to check my work schedule, and I'll be helping Chrissie out with the girls in between shifts.'

All of those feel-good endorphins which came from kissing Shona began to dissipate as she began erecting barriers between them. Until now she hadn't given any apparent thought to work or responsibilities. Something he'd been only too happy to go along with in the spirit of spontaneity and having fun.

'Reality's crashing in to spoil the party, huh?' It sucked, but they both had work and family to consider now they were back and he knew neither of them would purposely let anyone down.

She gave him a half-smile. 'We knew it couldn't last for ever.'

'No, but that doesn't mean it's over. Think of it as being on hold for now.' It was the only way he'd get through the days until they could be together again.

Shona touched her fingers to her lips, sure she could still feel Alasdair there. The smile which followed came easily, remembering that kiss before they'd parted last night. Yes, she'd had reservations about extending their relationship beyond one night in the cottage, but he'd done a good job of persuading her.

'Someone looks happy today,' one of her colleagues remarked as she began her shift at the hospital.

'I'm just in a good mood.' As she said it, Shona realised she was upbeat about the future for the first time since Iain's passing.

'Well, something or someone has put a spring in your step.' Sheila raised an eyebrow and gave her a knowing wink.

Shona neither confirmed nor denied her suspicions but Alasdair was definitely the reason for her good mood today. Of course, Chrissie had pounced the second she'd walked in the door last night, demanding to know everything. She mightn't have shared all the details of her time with Alasdair, but enough to have her sister literally bouncing with joy.

'Is this the real deal?' she'd asked, clutching Shona's hands, excited for her.

The direct question hadn't given her time to overthink anything and she'd answered as honestly as she could. 'Yes. I think so.'

Only to start another bounce around the living room, this time getting dragged along with her squealing sister. Finally admitting that she wanted to be with Alasdair was like the sun coming out after a rainy day. Her feelings were no longer clouded with worry because she knew being with him was all she wanted. She'd seen who he was and knew it was time to stop playing it safe. Take a chance on love for once.

She couldn't wait for her working day to be over so she could share how she felt about Alasdair with him in person. If possible, finally take him up on that offer of a sleepover.

A couple of hours into her shift they received word about an emergency coming into A&E. The waiting was the hardest part, knowing it could be a life-or-death situation coming in and being unable to do anything until the doors opened and the patients were wheeled in for treatment.

Then she heard someone mention lifeboat crew and she swore her heart stopped. 'Who is it?' she demanded someone tell her as her heart resumed beating. This time at an alarming rate as her stress levels soared sky-high. What if it was Alasdair? What if she'd wasted the time she'd had with him and now she'd never get to tell him how she felt about him? How she never wanted to imagine life without him?

'All we know is that several men have been hurt out at sea. One man with life-changing injuries.'

The news didn't help her calm down and she immediately tried phoning Alasdair to make sure he was all right. The unanswered ring tone caused the swell of anxiety inside to almost choke her.

So here she was, waiting to hear if the man she'd fallen for was seriously injured. Her worst nightmare come true. Heart pounding, palms sweating and on the verge of tears, she watched for the door opening and listened for the clatter of the trolley and paramedics rushing in. It was difficult not to think back to when she'd lost her father and the void it had left in her. That loss, the grief and the injustice of not having him anymore was something she'd never truly got over. She couldn't go through that again with Alasdair. Not when she'd only just opened her heart to let him in.

Shona barely heard the paramedic's assessment as the first stretcher came in, holding her breath until she could see the face of the patient.

'Adult male…thirties…serious injury…'

In among the bodies moving to transfer him to a hospital bed, she could see the flash of hi-vis gear. If she'd been thinking clearly she'd know that all the crew wore the same gear, as did most fishermen, but she wasn't. How could she be logical when her future could be dying in that bed?

Once the paramedics had left she stepped up to the side of the bed to help cut off the man's clothes. Her pulse was racing so fast and hard she was afraid she might faint if she found Alasdair hovering there between life and death. Whilst her hands continued to work and do everything her medical training had instilled in her, she was standing on tiptoe, trying to see the face smeared with blood and dirt.

It wasn't Alasdair. Her knees almost buckled in relief, then she quickly pulled herself back together to treat the unfortunate man who'd suffered terribly.

She worked on autopilot, doing everything she could for the best outcome, but thoughts of Alasdair weren't far from her mind. Then suddenly there he was, being pushed in on another trolley.

'Alasdair? What happened? Are you all right?' Once she was finished assisting with the first patient, she rushed over to his side to see what had happened.

'The skipper of the yacht we were called to hit some rocks and he suffered some crush injuries. That's who's in the other bed. It was rough out there and I had an argument with the tow line. I took a bit of a knock but I'm sure I'll be fine.' At least he was conscious but there was an alarming amount of blood everywhere. Including the dressing at his temple, which was scarlet now.

'You have a head injury. You'll need an X-ray at the very least.' Inside, she wanted to hug him, to throw herself upon him and thank the heavens for keeping him alive. Her emotions didn't translate so well outwardly. Her tone clipped and clinical.

'It's the other guy you should be worried about. I'm only here because the paramedics insisted I get checked over.' He was so calm about what had clearly been a serious incident she was close to shaking him.

'You know you can't ignore a head injury. There could be a concussion or something worse.' She hoped not but they couldn't take any chances.

'Hey, I'm fine. Don't worry.' He reached out to her but she refused to let him touch her and distract her from everything she was feeling right now.

'How can I not worry, Alasdair? Every time you go out in that boat I'm going to picture you getting hurt or never coming back.'

Her voice cracked as she tried to concentrate on cleaning the gash on his forehead. This was day one in the reality of being in a couple with him and she was already sick with nerves over his welfare. It couldn't possibly be healthy for either of them to sustain this level of anxiety over his work on a daily basis.

This time he caught hold of her wrist and forced her to look at him. 'I've been doing this for a long time. I don't take unnecessary risks.'

'But you do take necessary risks and you do get hurt. I'm sorry but I can't spend my life waiting and worrying every time you leave home.'

'I never asked you to.'

'No, but that's what would happen if we were in a relationship. I can't simply switch off my feelings when you walk out the door. Neither can I go through losing anyone else. I've only just got my life back on track.'

'I know you lost your father out there but he was on his own. I have my crew and I have experience. You should trust me to do my job and come back to you.'

'Sometimes it's not that simple. Fate doesn't always give you the choice whether to live or die. Iain was a fitness fanatic who never thought that he'd get sick but he did. He left me too.' The tears were pooling in her eyes now and she didn't intend to break down in front of her colleagues. She'd do what she had to do here and then she'd move on to her next patient. They could finish this conversation later in private, when things weren't so in the moment and emotionally charged.

'I'm not Iain and I'm not your father. You're not getting rid of me anytime soon, Shona.' He was trying to cheer her up but it wasn't going to work. Today had been a reality check for her, and losing Alasdair at sea was a very real possibility.

She'd been content with her lot here until he'd crashed into her life again. Her work at the hospital and life with Chrissie and the girls had been enough for her. There hadn't been any real stress. Alasdair had made her yearn for more but at too high a cost. The worry, and the hole he'd leave in her life and her heart, was too much to risk for a future which might never be theirs for the taking.

'We'll talk later. The doctor will be around soon, to organise any scans he wants and to stitch up that wound.' She went to leave, knowing she couldn't say more of what she had to say without breaking down, and that wouldn't look very professional to her colleagues or patients when they were in the middle of an emergency. Her personal crisis would simply have to be put on hold for now.

Alasdair sat up and swung his legs over the side of the bed. He was about to get up and follow her when he sat back down with a thump and closed his eyes.

'What are you doing? You're in no state to go

anywhere. Do as you're told and lie down until the doctor sees you.' Despite her desire to get away from him as quickly as possible, she knew Alasdair had to be careful with that head injury.

'Everything's spinning.'

'Lie down!' Her bossy nurse side came out, as it did for all stubborn patients who didn't know what was good for them. 'You could have a concussion.'

'I don't care about that. I'm more concerned about what's going on with us.' He was still talking as she lifted his legs back up onto the bed and pushed him firmly back down on to the pillows.

'That can wait until you can at least see straight. This is exactly what worries me, Alasdair. You give no thought for your own safety. That's fine if you're on your own but unacceptable for someone waiting at home for you. I just can't...' She walked away this time before she caused a scene in her workplace, or more than the one she'd already made.

This wasn't the place to end the best thing that had ever happened to her. She needed to do that where she had somewhere to hide later and cry herself into oblivion.

'Can I go now?' Alasdair was poised, ready to bolt as soon as he got the go-ahead. There were more important matters to deal with than a bump on the head. The sight of his blood had frightened Shona away and he needed to reassure her this wasn't about to become the norm.

He understood her concerns surrounding what he did for a living, and the baggage she had left over from her past. Goodness knew he had his own hang-ups or he wouldn't have waited so long before getting to know her again. Some old wounds never completely healed but he was sure with time they could both put those past hurts behind them. Shona was as different a person from his ex as he hoped he was from her late husband. It showed how much she cared about him—even if she refused to admit it—when the thought of him getting hurt frightened her so much. He'd be flattered if he wasn't sure she was about to end things. Before she began overthinking everything good they'd had together over these past days, he needed to persuade her that he was perfectly safe. Now he had her in his life, had someone to come home to, he certainly had no intention of risking it all in a moment of madness on the high seas.

'I'd rather you stayed here where we can keep an eye on you—' The doctor had run all the necessary checks and stitched the wound, so Shona could no longer use that as an excuse to avoid having the conversation they apparently needed to have.

'But I can go?' He was already on his feet.

'If you have any headaches, blurred vision or nausea—'

'Yes, I know, I'll have to come back.' With the all-clear he could put some of Shona's fears to rest. Though he was going to have a job with the others. A task he was willing to undertake when he knew they had something special to work towards.

That night at the cottage hadn't been a fluke. A romantic fantasy they'd confused for something more. Not when their day in the city had been equally fulfilling. He was eager to capitalise on that time they'd spent together now they were back home but he'd been able to sense Shona pulling away even last night. As though she didn't want what they had encroaching in any way on her home life. He, on the other hand, would be delighted to have her with him in every aspect of his existence. When he was with her, or at least knew they'd be together at some point, the loneliness he'd experienced over these past years no longer reared its ugly head.

'Is Nurse Kirk around?' he asked at the reception desk, certain they would know where to find her.

'You've just missed her. Her shift ended about

an hour ago.' Her smiling colleague gave him the vital information he needed for his mission.

'Thanks, I'll see if I can catch her.' It was typical of her, he thought, to stay on after she was due to go home, selflessly putting in the extra work to care for whoever needed her. He liked to think he was one of those people. That she would go the extra mile to give him another chance because he needed her.

He guessed she'd take the scenic route home, via the coastal path, where she'd have the sound of the sea to accompany her journey. Sure she wouldn't hang around in the cold weather, he jogged after her, ignoring the advice to take things easy after his hospital treatment.

When he was about three quarters of the way along the route to Shona's place, he spotted her in the distance. He'd know her anywhere, even swamped in her quilted winter coat, hood up to protect her from the wind. In their short time together he'd already developed some sort of homing device where she was concerned. As though he could sense her energy even from this distance away.

'Shona!' He tried calling out to her, but the wind carried her name out to sea, leaving him standing on the precipice alone. She didn't have very much further to walk, and he knew that if she got there first he wouldn't stand a chance.

There was no way she'd discuss her private life on the doorstep and frankly, he'd prefer to talk somewhere else too.

A rush of adrenaline spurred him on to a sprint, his thighs and lungs burning with the effort after everything else he'd been through today. If he thought it could keep her in his life he'd crawl to her on his hands and knees.

'Shona!' he yelled again, this time seeming to catch her attention. Her brisk pace halted as his increased. By the time he reached her and she turned around he was struggling for breath.

'Alasdair Murray, you really are the most insufferable man I've ever met. I suppose the doctor suggested you take up running to cure that head wound, did he?' The pursed lips and raised eyebrow would have been warning enough she wasn't pleased, even without the dreaded folded arms.

'Not exactly, but he did say there was no real damage.' He rapped his knuckles on his skull to show her it was still sound and intact. In theory.

'He probably also told you to go home and rest. Not charge around the island like a demented puppy.'

'I wanted to talk to you and show you I'm fine. None of us go through life without getting into a few scrapes here and there. Just because my job takes me out in a boat, it doesn't mean that some day I'm not going to return.' In his eyes she was being illogical. The sea was part of island life. It wasn't as if he could avoid it even if he did something else as a career.

'But it's a possibility. You have every right to do what you want but I'm sorry, today has reminded me why I should stay single.'

That last word hurt him more than the head injury. She was abandoning him because of who he was, thought him incapable of keeping his word. Another one in a line of people he'd never be good enough for just by being himself. It didn't matter how unintentional that was on Shona's part, that was how it felt, and he'd had enough experience of his trust being betrayed to recognise it. He didn't know if it was his body or soul which suddenly decided to concede to exhaustion, but he was regretting both leaving the hospital and running. Something he couldn't tell Shona for fear of confirming she was indeed better off without worrying about him.

'You know we have something good, Shona.' It was a plea for her to believe in him, in them, and not give up so easily. The relationship between them had always been special, even if at times they'd been too afraid to recognise it. This could be their last chance to grab that bit of happiness, and he for one didn't want anything to spoil it.

Except Shona was ducking her head so she was almost swallowed up between her hood and the scarf wrapped up around her mouth. It wasn't looking hopeful.

'We *had* something good. One night together. Perhaps that was all we were ever meant to have.'

He couldn't see into her eyes clearly enough to tell how serious she was but heard it in her voice. She was too cool, too calm, for this to be a knee-jerk reaction. He almost wished he'd never chased after her. If he'd stayed in that hospital bed at least he would have had that illusion that they were somehow still together. He wanted to fight for her and a future together but deep down he knew he shouldn't have to. If she didn't want to be with him he wasn't going to coax her into it. He'd made the mistake of falling for someone who clearly had never truly felt as strongly for him as he did for them, and he wasn't going to do it again. Even if it was killing him inside to accept her version of events.

'I don't believe that but if that's your way of saying it's over…' He threw up his hands, incapable of saying anything more without making a fool of himself. Instead, he turned and walked away, not knowing where he was going but certain it wasn't with Shona. He wouldn't stay where he wasn't wanted.

* * *

Shona's heart was in her throat as she watched Alasdair disappear up over the hill. He didn't turn back to look at her one last time, confirming that she'd well and truly got her point across. They were over. She sucked in a shaky breath and let it out again on a small cry of anguish. Losing Alasdair wasn't what she wanted but it was what she needed to do for self-preservation. So surely, now she'd dispatched him out of her life she should be standing tall, confident she'd done the right thing? Not so wobbly she wasn't sure her legs could carry her the short distance home?

She managed to get there by sheer willpower alone. Windswept and weeping on the hills was the sort of image she wanted to avoid. Certainly, it wouldn't help convince Alasdair that she'd meant what she'd said, and she needed him to believe it so he'd stay away. Her resolve was so weak where he was concerned, to the point where she'd lost her heart to him already, the more distance between them the better. Something that wasn't easy on a small island.

When she reached the house, she opened the door as quietly as she could and tried to sneak up the stairs unnoticed. Unfortunately, that one squeaky step which always gave the twins away also became her undoing.

'Shona? Is that you?' Chrissie appeared at the bottom of the stairs.

'Yeah. I think I'll just head to bed. I'm shattered.' She kept on walking up the stairs, only a few metres away from being able to grieve for her most recent loss in private.

'Stop.' Chrissie's authoritative voice and the sound of her footsteps on the stairs told Shona she'd been rumbled. 'What's wrong?'

'Nothing,' she mumbled into the scarf she still hadn't removed from around the bottom half of her face.

A hand on her shoulder forced her to turn around. Chrissie pulled the hood and scarf away so she could see her more clearly. 'You look like you're on the verge of tears. What's going on?'

A denial that anything was wrong was on the tip of her tongue, but the tears began before she could get the lie out. Instead, she was forced to confess what she'd done. 'I ended things with Alasdair.'

'Already? Last night the two of you looked as though you were going to devour each other on the doorstep. What has he done to upset you?' Her sister's loyalty was heart-warming, even if she was blaming the wrong person for stuffing things up.

'It wasn't Alasdair's fault,' Shona sighed and continued on to her bedroom with Chrissie following. She flopped onto her bed and lay staring up at the ceiling, wondering what she'd just done. Her reticence to talk didn't put Chrissie off. She simply threw herself onto the bed beside Shona, waiting for a girlie catch-up.

'Well, something has obviously happened and I'm here to listen. You've got to get used to the idea of sharing your problems, Sis. You're not on your own any more.' Chrissie nudged her with an elbow to remind her that that lonely period of her life was over. She still had family to turn to. That fuzzy thought only made her more emotional. Then she remembered Alasdair, who was on his own, save for a father who treated him dreadfully, and she felt worse than ever.

'He puts his life in danger for a living. I can't be with someone who doesn't value their own safety, or my state of mind. I've already lost a father and a husband, and I can't risk losing anyone else important in my life.'

'Okay, don't take this the wrong way, but don't you think you're being incredibly selfish?'

'What? How?' This wasn't quite the sisterly support Shona had been expecting. She thought sharing her problem was supposed to make her feel better, not worse.

'You're looking at this in completely the wrong way. Alasdair saves lives for a living. I'm sure he no more wants to lose his than you do. It's just an excuse you're using to push him away.' Chrissie was sitting up now, no longer relaxed for their supposed cosy sisterly chat.

'I'm pushing him away before he breaks my heart into a million pieces.' Although it had already kind of felt like that when she'd watched him walk away knowing they'd never have that night at the cottage together again.

'I would have thought it was too late for that. I can see by the look in your eyes when you talk about Alasdair the way that you feel about him. It seems to me that you're punishing both of you for no good reason. You deserve to be happy, Shona. That doesn't mean you have to remain single for the rest of your life.'

'What I went through after Dad, Mum, then Iain…it would kill me to have to go through that again.'

'I lost my parents and a partner too, or have you conveniently forgotten that? Okay, so mine walked out on me but it still left me devastated.'

'You have the girls,' Shona said meekly, re-alising she'd never considered how much her sister's circumstances were like her own. The only difference was that when Chrissie's partner had gone she'd had little ones who needed her, who gave her a reason to get up in the morning. Shona had literally been left on her own and had struggled to get out of bed.

'Do you think that made it easier? I was alone with two babies and terrified how I was ever going to cope, but you know what? Life has to go on. You can't hide away for ever, just in case something bad happens. That's no way to live, Shona. I'm sorry if I sound harsh but I'd give anything to have a man like Alasdair in my life. You're tossing him away because you're afraid of taking a chance on loving someone again. I never had you down as a coward, Sis.' Chrissie was on her feet now, hands on hips, pacing the room. Shona had never seen her so wound up, and currently felt like one of the twins having a stern telling off.

'I'm not. I'm just…careful.' It sounded pathetic even to her ears. She'd had the night of her life with Alasdair, followed by a fun day playing dress-up. He'd done nothing wrong but make her fall for him. She was the one who had the problem, but there was simply no way around her decision to split up with him. It wasn't the first time she'd had to get over Alasdair Murray, but she was no coward. This time she wasn't going to run away from the fallout. How could she when she still had her duties as Chief Elf to carry out?

CHAPTER TWELVE

'OKAY, CAROL SINGERS. Take your places around the Christmas tree for the lighting ceremony. Santa and Elf, you're the main attraction, so we want you to meet the ferry and lead people to the village square.' Eric, the committee chairman, allocated places to everyone gathered outside the community centre, his breath rising like chimney smoke into the frosty air.

It was the first time Alasdair had been near Shona since that day of the accident. He was surprised she'd agreed to still do this and knew it was going to be hard being together all night without thinking about what could have been. Or what had already been. These past few days had been bad enough not seeing or talking to her. He had no appetite, couldn't sleep, and was tormented by thoughts of what he'd done wrong. It was the after-effects of a bad break-up without actually getting the benefit of being with Shona long term.

'It's good to see you, Shona. I'm sure you're freezing out here in this weather.' It was awkward, standing together making small talk after their last encounter, but he needed some sort of coping mechanism to get through the rest of the night.

She gave him a hint of a smile. 'I've deployed the secret weapon: thermals.'

'Good idea. There are some perks to being Santa. Plenty of insulation.' He patted his fat suit, which covered a lot more than her skimpy elf costume. Not that he was really in the mood for being jolly. His Christmas would consist of him and a microwave turkey dinner in front of the TV as usual. However, this year he suspected he'd feel the loneliness more than ever, knowing what he could have had. If things had worked out he could have been waking up next to her on Christmas morning. That definitely wasn't happening, and though she hadn't formally withdrawn her invitation to celebrate with her and her family, given the circumstances...

'Shall we take our positions, then?' She wasn't hanging around, already a couple of steps ahead of him, apparently keen to get on with the job at hand. Probably to get it over with as quickly as possible so she wouldn't have to deal with him again.

'Try and stop me.' He let her lead the way

when she seemed so desperate to keep a distance between them. It would be interesting to see how she maintained that the rest of the evening when they were supposed to be working as a team.

To be honest he was still confused about what exactly had happened between them. Shona was a nurse. She saw the results of much worse accidents at work herself and was compassionate with her patients. Though she'd been concerned with his injuries, it had still prompted her to dump him. Not the bedside manner he'd expected or wanted. Clearly, she'd been looking for a way out and he'd presented her with the perfect excuse by feeding her fears.

The walkway down to the meeting point was lit by strings of fairy lights. In other circumstances it would have been quite romantic, huddled up together under the warm glow of the coloured lights. Shona, however, was choosing to stand on the opposite side of the path to him, stamping her feet to keep warm and waiting anxiously for the visitors to join them. It was a far cry from their night alone when they hadn't wanted anyone disturbing them.

'Here they come. I'll lead the first group and you can follow with the rest.' Her enthusiasm to get away from him only made his heart ache more.

'If that's what you want,' he said without a trace of the joviality expected of someone in his position. 'Merry Christmas, everyone. If you want to follow me, I'll take you to the heart of our wonderful Winter Wonderland.' Shona, on the other hand, had taken to her role with glee. It was definitely the chirpiest he'd ever seen her, and as she took the arm of an elderly gentleman to escort him to the square Alasdair had a moment of irrational jealousy. Something he was going to have to get over if he couldn't convince her to give him another chance.

Suddenly, the true nature of the island hit home. If she did meet someone new he'd be forced to see them around and his heart would take a repeat battering, facing the reality of the rejection time and time again.

When he tore his eyes away from Shona's delectable backside, he had a queue of expectant visitors staring at him. It was time to get the show on the road.

He rang his handbell and bellowed a 'Ho, ho, ho.'

All the faces immediately lit up as the magic of Christmas apparently unfurled before them. Alasdair thought it a shame his own belief in the miracle of the season was wavering. It was going to be a very long night. Not to mention a more miserable Christmas than usual.

Only the amazing memories they'd created in such a short space of time kept him going. Otherwise, he might begin to think he'd have been better off if they hadn't hooked up. At least then he wouldn't have known what he was missing out on now.

The sweet smell of chocolate enticed Shona over to one of the nearby stalls, where she was surprised to see Chrissie serving the hot drinks.

'What are you doing here?'

'I'm just covering for Mrs Rose. She wanted to take the girls on the slide.' She poured some hot chocolate into a takeaway cup for Shona.

Shona glanced over at the field where they'd set up giant inflatable ice slides. Families were queuing up to take their turn sliding down in coloured dinghies, their collective delight both audible and visible as their breathy squeals hung like tufts of cotton candy in the night sky.

'I'm sure they'll love that. Can you give me another one of those, please?'

'For Alasdair? Feel free to put in a word for me if he's on the market again.' Chrissie wolf whistled, reminding her of everything she was throwing away.

Shona knew she was winding her up. That was what little sisters did. It didn't stop the surge of jealousy rising inside, making her nauseous at the thought. Alasdair was free to see whoever he wanted and that was entirely down to her. It shouldn't bother her who showed an interest in him, or vice versa, but it did. She ignored the comment rather than dwell on it any longer, letting her imagination torment her.

'I should take these back before our customers start queuing.'

'They're lighting the tree soon. Will we see you down there?'

'Maybe.' Shona didn't make any promises, unsure if she could stand her sister or any of the other interested parties making doe eyes at Alasdair. Dressed as Santa or not, he drew female attention, and watching it in action made her uncomfortable. Probably because she still thought of him as hers.

She made her way over to the grotto where they were to spend the remainder of the night together.

'Something to warm you up, Mr Claus,' she said, handing one of the cups over to Alasdair. Their fingers brushed as he took it from her but neither of them pulled away. She missed his touch along with everything else about him.

'Thanks. Santa's freezing his baubles off in here.' His joke interrupted the awkward atmosphere and made her laugh. Something else she would miss going forward without him. Perhaps their sense of humour hadn't matured beyond those teenage sweethearts teasing each other down on the beach. Whatever it was, Alasdair always managed to bring out her fun side and make her feel young again.

She'd managed a life without him before, but it seemed boring in comparison these days. Now she was back to being nurse, sister, auntie and babysitter. No longer Alasdair's Chief Elf, sex goddess and sparring partner. The New Year would be off to a depressing start in comparison to what she'd experienced with him these past weeks, and she had no one to blame but herself.

They took up their places as the excitable children rushed in to get their gifts from Santa. It was a lovely thing to be part of making a little one's day special, but it was tough on her watching Alasdair being so kind to everyone who walked in through the tinsel-covered doors. Every crying infant he soothed with a soft reassurance and each lengthy wish list he listened to with interest only reaffirmed what she already knew. He was an amazing, warm man who would make a fabulous father one day. Exactly what she wanted in a partner but had been too afraid to commit to. Unfortunately, she wasn't any happier being on her own, and didn't think about him or his safety any less.

As the next family came through the grotto

Shona took the little girl's hand and led her to the only person everyone here was interested in meeting.

'I'm Shona. What's your name?'

'Leesa.' She looked shyly up at Shona as she scuffed her shoes on the ground. Not all kids were eager to bounce onto Santa's lap for a chat, with some finding the whole experience a little overwhelming. It was Shona's job to put them at ease before they reached Santa to avoid any tears. At the end of the day they all wanted to walk away with a present, and Shona and Alasdair, along with the parents, wanted it to be a happy occasion.

'And how old are you, Leesa?' asked Shona.

'Five.' She looked back at her parents, who were waving from the door and encouraging her to go and speak to Santa.

'Oh, a big girl. Santa will have to find you a big girl's present, won't he?'

Leesa nodded, her initial hesitation waning at the prospect. Now she seemed more comfortable, Shona helped her on to Santa's lap for the all-important present discussion.

'Santa, this is Leesa. She's five years old.'

Alasdair shook the child's hand, already sure to be making her feel important. 'Hello, Leesa. Have you been a good girl this year?'

Leesa nodded without hesitation.

'And what would you like Santa to bring you on Christmas morning?'

'I want a baby doll and a pram, please, Santa.'

'Well, with such lovely manners, how could I refuse?' Alasdair looked to the parents, who gave him a thumbs-up from the doorway. Shona's heart melted a little more with every interaction she watched in the grotto, fast becoming a sentimental puddle rather than a functioning organ she was trying to protect.

'I think my little helper might have something special for you.' He reminded Shona that she was supposed to be assisting here tonight instead of mooning and brooding over what could have been if only she were a tad braver. If she weren't so frightened by the thought of losing him, she could have a future including Alasdair and children of her own. She was relatively young and still wanted a family. Alasdair was the only one she could picture raising children with and she was beginning to realise it was all an unnecessary sacrifice.

Why on earth was she denying herself the chance to have it all? The clouds of doubt and worry were beginning to clear, so she could see what they'd been obscuring all this time. A chance to be happy. No one knew what the future was going to bring but surely it was about time she lived her life the way she wanted.

She'd settled for the safe option once before and, though she'd been content at the time, it was apparent she hadn't been fulfilling her heart's desire. Perhaps it was about time she took back control of her life instead of hiding. She could only hope it wasn't too late to have everything she really wanted.

'This one's for you, Leesa.' She handed over a wrapped parcel she knew had a small stuffed dog inside, sure it had a safe home with its new owner. To keep her mind off Alasdair she'd spent her spare time helping buy age-appropriate gifts and wrapping them for the grotto. It had given her some idea of what it would be like gearing up for Christmas and shopping for her own children. The magic of the season was still there for her in watching the joy on other people's faces as they opened their gifts. Minus the elf outfit, she could see herself doing this with Alasdair on an annual basis.

Leesa hopped down off Santa's knee and ran towards her parents, clutching her present.

'Merry Christmas,' Shona and Alasdair chorused after her.

'They're lighting the tree soon. We should probably make an appearance.' Alasdair was out of the door before she had a chance to talk to him. He walked away so quickly it was impossible for her to catch up in her elf shoes in order to mend some bridges. The jingling bells on her feet sounded the death knell for her heart. It shouldn't come as any surprise that he didn't want to be anywhere near her when she'd pushed him away. Using his job as an excuse to prevent her from getting hurt again. Ironic when she was hurting more than ever without him.

The choir had started singing sentimental Christmas carols as people gathered around the tall, full Norwegian spruce in the centre of the village. It had even begun to snow. Everything was so beautiful and perfect it was overwhelming for someone who was so unbearably sad. By the time she joined everyone else she was barely holding back the sobs stuck in her throat. She'd really messed everything up by letting him go, but it didn't seem fair on Alasdair to tell him she'd changed her mind. As though he were an item on a menu she could take or leave depending on her appetite. He deserved better than that. As always, she'd simply have to live with her life choices and the mistakes she'd made along the way.

'You okay?' Chrissie was standing at the edge of the crowd with the girls, waiting for the lights.

She forced a smile and nodded enthusiastically, almost shaking out the tears welling in her eyes. Thankfully, the chairman took the mic at that point and distracted Chrissie from analysing her too much.

'Okay, everyone. Let's start the countdown. Five, four, three, two, one...'

The tree came to life, the colourful bulbs lifting the gloom and instigating a round of applause interspersed with 'ooh's and 'ah's. Shona stared up at the full branches hung with glittering baubles and sparkling tinsel, wishing the rest of her world felt so shiny and happy.

A tug on her tunic alerted her to a child trying to get her attention. She expected to see one of the twins and was surprised to find the little girl from earlier smiling at her.

'Thank you,' she said, cuddling the toy dog she'd received as a present.

It was enough for Shona to break out of her self-pity for a moment. 'You're welcome, Leesa.'

She watched as the child skipped back towards her parents, only to see her turn in the other direction and start running. 'Santa!'

Everything seemed to happen in slow motion after that. Leesa was fixated on Alasdair, who was waiting to cross the road. She didn't see the lorry reversing down the street, but Alasdair did. He ran out to grab her away and the screech of brakes pierced the night. The throng of people moving away from the tree blocked her view now, but the resulting gasps and murmurs made her fear the worst.

'Alasdair!' Shona screamed and ran to where she'd seen them last.

Leesa's mother had her tearful daughter in her arms and thankfully she looked unharmed. The relief was short-lived as she realised Alasdair must have pushed her out of the path of the truck and taken the hit himself. She swore her own heart stopped as she fought past everyone rubbernecking at the scene. When she saw Alasdair standing talking to the pale lorry driver, she couldn't control herself and launched at him in a flood of tears.

'Hey, I'm all right,' he whispered against her neck, but she couldn't stop crying.

They weren't together, but she knew in that moment if something had happened to him she'd regret not having been brave enough to be honest with him. Whatever fate had in store, she couldn't change it any more than she could change her feelings for him.

'Why don't we go somewhere private? I don't want to upset any kids.' Trust Alasdair to be thinking of others when he'd just had a near miss with the rear end of a lorry. That was just him. He was always going to save people whatever the cost to him personally and she knew that was something rare and special which should be celebrated. She was the one being selfish, wanting him all to herself. Wrapping someone like Alasdair up in cotton wool was never going to work. It wasn't fair to him or anyone else who benefitted from having him in their lives. She would either have to learn to live with his career choice or lose him for ever, and tonight had shown her that wasn't possible. With or without him, he was always going to be on her mind.

He took her by the hand and she let him lead her to the grotto, away from any children who might have witnessed her outburst. Once inside the little wooden hut, he closed the door and turned to face her.

'Now, do you mind telling me what all that was about?' He was smiling, obviously amused by her little outburst. Her reaction to Alasdair's accident had been over the top, but it served to prove the strength of her real feelings for him. There was no getting away from that no matter how hard she tried.

'I was afraid I'd lost you.'

'Yeah?' He seemed surprised by that, and no wonder when she'd behaved so erratically to-wards him recently.

'Of course. I care about you, Alasdair.' It was a big admission for her after the lengths she'd gone to trying to convince herself and everyone else otherwise.

'And that's a problem because…?' He was going to make her spell this out, so it was clear to both of them exactly what she wanted.

'I can't stand the thought of you getting hurt. Or worse.' Even now she was choked up, reliving the moment she thought he'd been hit by the truck.

He didn't say anything at first, but removed his hat and beard, so it was Alasdair she was having this heart-to-heart with and not a blue-eyed Father Christmas. It made it easier to face the emotions she'd been trying to hold at bay for so long.

He wrapped his arms around her waist and pulled her closer. 'Everyone feels that way about the people they love. Don't you think I worry about you too? But I want to be with you, Shona, and that's more important than hiding behind any irrational fear. I love you. I always have.'

She closed her eyes and let the words wash over her. Alasdair loved her and she loved him. Their fate together had been sealed at seventeen and she'd been running from it for far too long.

'I love you too,' she whispered.

His lips pressed gently against hers to seal the bond for ever. 'Then can we stop being silly and just be together? That's all I want.'

'Me too.' At this moment in time nothing else mattered than being with Alasdair and having a future together to look forward to.

EPILOGUE

One year later

'FINN, GET OUT of the presents.' Shona lifted the small border terrier away from the Christmas tree. He'd been a surprise from Alasdair to keep her company during those long nights when he was out on a call. An attempt to stop her worrying.

'Do you need me to do anything?' Chrissie popped her head around from the kitchen door to see what all the commotion was in the living room.

'If you and the girls can keep him entertained, we can get on with making dinner.' She and Alasdair had volunteered to host Christmas this year for Chrissie and the girls. That had been pre-puppy, and although everyone loved him, and vice versa, he was proving to be a handful.

'No problem. These two are trying to talk me into getting one for us as well, but I think we've enough chaos going on without throwing a mischievous puppy into the mix.'

'So, presents or dinner first?' Alasdair appeared from the smoky depths of the kitchen, where Chrissie had had a mishap with the roast potatoes before they'd convinced her they could manage without her contribution.

'Presents!' the twins chimed.

Shona glared at him. He'd known perfectly well that the children would want to open their gifts before sitting down at the dining room table. He was like a big kid himself, but she couldn't blame him for wanting to go all out this year. It was a special time for him more than everyone else to have a family around him, celebrating the season together and showing their love and appreciation for each other. He was excited, and in turn he was making the day more special for all of them.

Shona had moved in with him not long after the previous Christmas, willing to take that chance on love when the alternative seemed so much more unbearable. Nothing stopped her worrying about him, but then, she worried about her sister and her nieces too. That was part of her nature and he accepted it. She'd just have to do the same when it came to his job.

'You're only saying that because you can't wait to open your own,' she teased, when he was already kneeling by the tree distributing the gifts he'd bought. It was a wonder she hadn't been asked to don the elf costume again this year for the job.

The girls and Chrissie loved having him in their lives almost as much as Shona did. He was like a big brother to everyone, and it helped that he could cook. They never went hungry at family get-togethers, which had become pretty frequent.

'This one's for Tilly,' he said, and lifted out a huge, odd-shaped parcel from behind the tree. An identical one was given to Marie.

'You really shouldn't have, Alasdair,' Chrissie protested weakly, but Shona knew she was happy there was someone else looking out for her children. Once again, she thought about what a great dad he would make some day. They'd talked about having children of their own and she was sure it would happen at some point. It was all about the timing and would happen when they were both ready. She just hoped that time was coming soon. It was occasions such as this which only made her broody about the future and having a family of their own. Alasdair was equally keen but he'd made a point of saying he wanted to be sure their children had a more stable background than he'd ever had. She assumed that meant marriage and everything that commitment entailed, and though it was still relatively early days for them, they were pretty solid as a couple.

'It's no problem. I loved every minute getting to pick out presents for them. And you two. This one's for you, Chrissie.'

Shona swore her sister actually blushed when he presented her with a small, exquisitely wrapped gift. It had been a long time since any man had done anything remotely kind for her and Shona hoped she too would find her soulmate some time soon.

She didn't waste any time ripping off the paper to reveal a small jewellery box.

'I'm not sure if I should be jealous or not of my boyfriend buying jewellery for my little sister,' she teased them both, not in the least bit miffed at sharing this wonderful man with her family.

'It's gorgeous.' Chrissie discarded paper and box in her excitement to get at the contents. She hung the gold chain around her neck and held the locket open so Shona could see what was inside. 'It's the girls,' she said, tears welling in her eyes.

'That's so thoughtful, Alasdair.' Even Shona was surprised by the lengths he'd gone to in order to make Chrissie's day. Though she shouldn't be after all this time of living with the man who proved to her every day what an amazing person he was.

'Thank you, Alasdair.' He was suddenly mobbed by Chrissie and the girls, who launched themselves at him for a group hug. Finn bounded in on top of them until they all landed on the floor in a giggling heap. The pup had no idea what was going on, but they were all so happy that his little tail was wagging non-stop and he was licking the faces of everyone within reach.

Shona was beginning to feel a little left out. She gave an exaggerated cough. 'I don't mean to spoil the party but aren't you forgetting someone?'

Normally presents weren't that important to her, and she much preferred to do the giving than the receiving, but this was their first Christmas living together and she was excited about what special thing he'd got her too.

'Am I?' He looked at the girls with a puzzled look, teasing her right back.

'Auntie Shona!' they chorused before collapsing into another fit of giggles.

'Oh, yes. There might be something here, right at the back of the tree.' Alasdair made a big deal of scrabbling about on the floor, as though he'd lost her gift. She wasn't so easily fooled but the anticipation was getting to such astronomic levels she was worried it might not live up to her expectations. The others had all received such thoughtful gifts, she hoped he hadn't bought her something more practical, like a household appliance or something equally unromantic.

'It doesn't matter if you all want to go through and get started on dinner.' Her reaction was a mixture of her fear about being disappointed and ungrateful, and an urgency to eat before the food all got cold.

'Don't be silly. As if I would leave you out.' He produced another small gift and held a sprig of mistletoe above her head to kiss her on the cheek before he handed it over.

'Thank you.' That warm feeling of being loved spread throughout her body, sure beyond all reason now that she would love whatever he'd given her. She already had the most precious thing he could share with her, his heart, and that meant the world to her.

She tried not to tear at the paper even though every instinct in her body was telling her to shred it already and get to the good stuff. It was important for her to relish every single second of this because she knew it would never happen again. Their first gift exchange was to be cherished and remembered for ever.

The small navy-blue velvet box she revealed made her heart soar along with her pulse. She dared not believe what she thought might just be lying inside. Carefully, she opened the box and the sparkle of diamonds almost blinded her. Not to mention brought a tear to her eye.

She covered her gasp with a hand, and when she saw Alasdair kneeling on the floor again he'd taken off the Santa hat and was reaching out a hand to her.

'Shona Kirk, will you do me the honour of being my wife?' His eyes, so full of love and emotion, were almost her undoing but made her certain of her answer.

'Yes. A thousand times, yes.' She let him slide the ring onto her finger as Chrissie and the twins shouted and clapped. It was a moment she was glad he'd chosen to share with her family.

He jumped up and pulled her into a hug before planting a long, sensual kiss on her lips. 'I can't wait to marry you and for us to have a family together. This seemed like the perfect time to start the journey.'

Shona nodded, afraid that if she spoke she'd become a sodden mess from the happy tears. It was all perfect. She had the man of her dreams and was back where it had all begun. On Braelin Island. Home.

* * * * *